Boo!

David Haynes

Copyright © David Haynes 2016. All Rights Reserved. No part of this document may be reproduced without written consent from the author

Edited by
Storywork Editing Services

Cover artwork by
Go on Write

Formatting by
Polgarus Studio

To find out more about David Haynes and his books visit his Blog
http://davidhaynesfiction.weebly.com/
or follow him on twitter
@Davidhaynes71

*For Sarah, George and our own
fearless greyhound, Tommy.*

1

Maldon Williams was nine years old when he saw a clown murder his parents. The clown used a kitchen knife to cut their throats from ear to ear, and blood dripped down the walls in thick, oozing rivers. Apart from his birthday party, that was the only thing Maldon remembered about being nine.

Mum had kicked and thrashed, her slippered feet sliding and slipping on the bloody floor, but Dad had been silent. Other than the sound of his gurgled last breath, he had not made a sound. Perhaps it was the shock.

The clown had seen Maldon, watching like that in the doorway. How could he miss him?

"Boo!" the clown said and smiled, his grin impossibly wide. A bubble of blood burst on the tip of his bright red nose and sprayed like a snotty sneeze all over Maldon's face.

Then the clown had left, as quickly and quietly as he came in. He walked out of the door with his frizzy orange wig bouncing on his head like a dreamy cloud.

And all the time, the carnival music played in Maldon's ears. Just like in the big top when the clowns rode their tiny bicycles and threw pies at each other. It played and it played.

*

It had been a very long time until Maldon felt able to look at, or even think about, a clown again. But then he read a book that truly changed his life. That book brought him here tonight. It led him to this very place. It invited him to meet the killer clown and to take back something the clown had stolen from him on that night. His smile.

"Now then, Bingo, where shall we begin?" Maldon sat on the chair opposite the clown and opened up the book.

Bingo couldn't answer, of course, because he had a ball gag in his mouth. He couldn't move either. The rope made sure of that.

"Sorry, you'll just have to be a mime clown tonight." He lifted the book and looked at the cover. It was as awful as it was wonderful. The needle teeth, the festering dark cavern of the clown's mouth and the hideous bloody diamonds around his eyes were hypnotic. He turned it around and showed it to his restrained clown. Their faces were slightly different. He didn't have the needle teeth for one and his hair was more red than orange, but Maldon knew he was in the right place. He had the right clown.

"This is my copy, one of the early editions. One of the best covers, I think." He could feel an excited buzz zipping through his body. It wasn't just the impending atrocity he was about to commit. No, just talking about the book gave him an intoxicated dizziness that came from nothing else. Nothing man-made or otherwise came close to it.

He smiled and looked over at Bingo's bookcase. "But you probably already knew that. I must admit to being a little envious, Bingo. Five copies! You have five copies of the book and all of them signed by Ben Night himself! It's incredible. Ahead of its time, that's what it was. Everyone's doing it now but back then putting a 'z' at the end of the word 'clown' made it stand apart. Gave it an edge. A nasty, sharp and jagged edge too!"

Bingo wriggled and made more grunting noises in response. Maldon wasn't surprised that Bingo was trying to join in the conversation, he was clearly a huge fan.

He turned the book around and looked at the cover again. It was that which had first attracted him to the book, or more accurately, stunned him into picking it up.

It had been on the book trolley, right at the bottom, but as he trawled through the dog-eared and slightly sticky collection of thrillers, he found himself staring into the eyes of his parents' killer. Right down to the droplet of blood on the end of its nose. It was a face he had been trying hard *not* to remember ever since, but it was one even drugs couldn't entirely obliterate.

And here he was. The killer clown from the kitchen. As bold as brass on the cover of a book.

"Pick one, Mouldy," the guard had said. *"Time to go beddy-byes."* And he had taken Clownz back to his cell and read it for as long as the light stayed on. Even when they

turned off the lights, he tried to read some more.

In the book, Sparkles The Clown travelled up and down the country slitting throats and eating the part of the brain that made people laugh. It wasn't much more than a chewy lump of gristle but inside it was the unimaginable power of smile. Eating it kept the painted smile on Sparkles's face and it kept his nose the brightest red imaginable. Some people had a better sense of humour than others, some were quicker to laugh and others barely knew how to smile. But children loved to laugh all the time. They were especially delicious and they made his smile run from ear to ear and his nose drip with blood.

It was no surprise that Bingo loved the same book. He had, after all, stolen Maldon's smile in just the same way.

How many times had he read that book? Too many to count. He'd read all of Ben Night's books more than twice but Clownz at least twenty times. It was never very far away from him.

When people said that books *spoke* to them, they were right. From the moment Maldon read the book, he had been utterly and horrifically transfixed by Sparkles. But it wasn't until a short time ago that the book had changed from being a graphic piece of fiction into something else. It had become his inspiration, his instruction manual and his reason for living. Why he hadn't considered it earlier was irrelevant. From that moment on, from the moment the thought crystallised itself and attached its wiry tendrils onto his brain, he knew what he must do. He had to kill the clown who had taken his smile. The clown called Bingo.

He shook his head. How he had found the book, how Sparkles had inspired him, barely mattered. Bingo was here, in front of him; the clown who had stolen his smile and kept it for his own. If it weren't for the book, he wouldn't be here now.

He stood up and pressed the tip of the knife to the clown's cheek.

"My smile is in there somewhere and I want it back. You killed them!"

Bingo grunted. It was all he could do.

In the days when heroin had been king, Maldon had been a good burglar. Not so good that he never got caught but good enough to get away with hundreds before the police finally got hold of him. He'd been a bit rusty, but breaking into the clown's house was easy. An unsecure kitchen window, a little shimmy through and then it was just a matter of waiting for him to come home.

The look on Bingo's face when he saw someone waiting behind the door was priceless. He could have laughed at that himself but he hadn't, he'd just said, "Boo!" and held the kitchen knife up for emphasis. Bingo went on and on about money. Even as he was being tied up, he was talking about how much he had and where it was. It was boring and Maldon tuned it out. All he was thinking about was how it would feel to smile again.

He leaned in closer and looked at the paint on the clown's face. Even though he was in control, just being so close to a clown made his stomach flutter with nerves. The white paint wasn't quite as bright as it had been earlier. Tears had made two dirty-looking ravines in his cheeks and his big, red smile wasn't quite as wide any more, but he was still a clown. A murdering, laughter-eating clown.

"What are you without this mask, I wonder? What lies beneath the mask of a clown?" He traced the tip of the knife down the bridge of the clown's nose. "Shall we find out?"

Bingo started to struggle. His voice was nothing but a muffled series of grunts and his body swayed from side to side as he tried to tip the chair over.

*

Maldon was forced to kill Bingo before he finished removing his mask. He had struggled so much that the mask started to get untidy around the edges. He threw it onto the floor and it landed with a slap.

He stood back and closed his eyes. He was waiting for the smile that had been taken from him all those years ago to magically return. Taking the clown's mask was the only thing that could bring it back. It had to be. Yet as he stood there, he felt no different. He touched his lips. They were still the same lifeless lumps of flesh they had always been. Where was it? Why hadn't it returned? A terrible sense of deflation washed over him. It wasn't supposed to feel like this.

He put Clownz back in his holdall, along with his bloody gloves, overalls and a selection of Bingo's clown costumes. He didn't know why he wanted to take them, he just did. It felt right.

He took a few steps toward the kitchen and admired his

wall art. A pattern of blood not dissimilar to the one in his parents' kitchen.

"Boo!" He smiled as he spoke the word. He'd written it with the tip of the knife and used the blood like ink. It was a bit scratchy but it was okay. It was Sparkle's catchphrase in the book when he was in the act of slicing someone's face off.

Was that someone laughing? He cocked his head and waited. No, it was just someone outside on the street. He started walking again and the laughter came through once more, only it was louder. And closer.

He turned around. There was nobody here except him and Bingo, what was left of him anyway.

"Hello?"

The laughter came back as a reply. *"You got me, Maldon. You got me good and proper."*

He took a step forward, toward the discarded mask, and bent down. Bingo's face lay on the blood-spattered carpet, looking up at him with hollow eyes. Where his nose should have been was just a jagged hole.

"Are you talking to me?" As he stared into the dark pools where his eyes should have been, the faint tinkle of carnival music filtered through. It was beautiful.

"You bet I am! Now get me off this filthy carpet and take me home."

Maldon fell back. The clown's lips had moved. Those big, red, banana-shaped lips had moved in time with the words. Yet how could this be?

"You... you took my childhood away from me, you destroyed everything!"

"That was him, not me. I'm hurt you don't recognise me! It's me, Sparkles. Your best buddy, Sparkles! You can't just leave me here now you've liberated me. Please take me home, Maldon. I'm tired."

Maldon opened his mouth to reply and then stopped. The music was louder again and the tune was terribly off-key. It was hideous yet hypnotic.

"I promise not to eat your brains out. I'm not sure you've got much fun inside you anyway. I reckon you might make me cry, not laugh, but I can help you change that. You'll smile again, Maldon."

"I have got fun inside me. I can laugh like everyone else!" He tried to laugh but he didn't know how.

"Pathetic! Take me home and we'll have some real fun."

"We will?" Maldon felt like a child.

"Sure we will. Reeeeeaaaallll fun!"

Maldon pushed himself back up and touched Sparkles. He expected the mask to be cold but it felt warm, almost hot. The music blared briefly in his ears. It really was him. It was really Sparkles.

"There, that's better. In the bag and off we go."

He cradled Sparkles and lowered him gently into the bag. There was a muffled grunt and then the circus music was gone.

"Steady on there, my man. You'll have me all battered and bruised!"

Maldon felt a strange sensation in his throat. It was as if something was trying to force its way out of him. Was it laughter?

He hummed along with the music. It had been a long time since it played in his ears like this. A very long time. He missed it terribly.

2

Ben Night hated selfies and not just because they made him look old. He hated them because getting that close to someone he didn't know made him itch. Bumping heads with someone who had obvious hair-hygiene issues made him want to vomit. It probably meant there were other hygiene issues too. But he couldn't afford to think about those *other* issues when he was having his photo taken. No, that would give him the look of someone about to cry. As well as someone with a double chin.

"Done?" he asked the boy. He was sure there had been two clicks of the camera already.

"One more," the boy replied and gave the camera a thumbs-up sign. Ben did the same and pulled away. The boy's hair smelled of fried food, onions and stale sweat. He walked away without saying anything else. He was staring at his phone.

"My pleasure," he whispered.

"Pleased to meet you, Mr Night." The next fan offered

her hand and he took it. Now this was more like it. What was she? Twenty-five, a little older maybe but at least twenty years younger than him.

"Pleased to meet you. Shall I sign your book?" he asked.

She blushed slightly and slid it across the table. "Could you make it out to Fleur, please?

He opened her copy of 'Howl' and started writing.

"You gave me nightmares for weeks after reading this. It's why I started writing."

Ben looked up. "Really? That's great to hear. I did a good job then." He carried on writing.

'To Fleur, maybe one day you'll give me nightmares. Ben.'

He slid it across the table to her. She read the inscription and immediately smiled. She really was very pretty.

"Selfie?" he asked.

"I hate them," she replied. "They always make me look bad."

Wasn't that typical? "Me too."

There was silence for a moment and then Ben spoke again. "Well it was nice meeting you, Fleur, and thank you for reading my books." He offered his hand again and noticed the absence of a ring on her left hand.

She took it. "And thank you for the message. I'll treasure it." She smiled and walked away.

Ben watched her go. Her long blonde hair swung with each step. It was so long it hung right down to her...

"Hello, Ben!"

He looked back, slightly startled by the interruption to his thoughts. A round-faced teenager with bad acne was smiling down at him and had his hand in a bag of pork scratchings.

"I love selfies!" he announced and reached into his pocket.

*

He stood in the shower and waited for the steam to open his pores to scrub away the afternoon. Book signings were good for half an hour, but after that the joy of the occasion wore off very quickly. He loved his readers, he loved each and every one of them – at a distance. On the end of an email or a letter was great, but not so much in person. There had been one exception today. The blonde girl, Fleur, had been pretty, very pretty and also *very* out of his league.

He climbed out and dried himself. One good thing about hotel rooms was that the towels were always clean. You didn't have to worry about washing them. Maybe he should move into a hotel, permanently.

All he wanted now was to have something to eat, drink a couple of beers and sleep. He needed to get home early tomorrow, collect Stan and get back to work. He had a couple of ideas that wouldn't keep quiet, and he wanted to get them down before they felt he was ignoring them and ran away. He hated that thought. Imagining that those little magic lights could just slip away, out of his head, and find another writer's head to fizz into.

There had been a time when all he had to do was sit at his desk and listen to those little sparks zipping around like tiny fireflies in his head. Each one carrying a little light bulb with *idea* etched on the side. Two or three of them would get together and pretty soon there would be hundreds of them bumping into each other, burning like the sun. That's where the books came from.

You couldn't write a book if those little fireflies died before they found their mate, though. If their wings fell off, they just fell to the floor like dirty bluebottles, buzzing and black. The carpet in his office was covered in thousands of little black corpses that only he could see.

Ben dressed quickly, picked up his book and went downstairs to the restaurant. Hotels like this served the same sort of food wherever you went. Steak, chicken or, if you were lucky, a mixed grill. He wanted steak, a great big juicy lump of meat, and some good chips on the side. All washed down with a couple of bottles of cold lager. Just what the doctor ordered. Especially when his agent was paying for it.

The restaurant/bar was quiet which was good. He didn't particularly like eating late but it allowed the fans time to clear out and give him some peace. He strolled across to the bar and ordered a bottle of lager, then took it to a table by the window and looked at the menu. Curry, lamb shank, mixed grill, Hunter's chicken and ah, there we go, 12oz rib-eye steak.

He put the menu down and looked out of the window.

It was dark outside and there were people milling about, waiting for taxis or dates or just for something to happen. It wasn't very interesting so his focus shifted onto his own reflection. That was a little more interesting but not in a particularly pleasing way. He looked old, older than he was.

Fairly soon the publisher was going to have to change the photograph in his books. That picture showed how Ben looked ten years ago. On a good day.

He looked away. The silver strands in his hair were dazzling.

"What can I get for you, sir?"

A boy-band waiter stood over him with a pen at the ready.

"A medium rib-eye please. And another one of these too, thanks." He held his bottle up and the waiter nodded then walked away.

Now, he also felt older than he looked, if that was at all possible. He finished the bottle and opened his book. He never went anywhere without one but he seldom read books by his peers in the horror genre any longer. It scared him how good they all were. In his opinion, much better than him by a country mile. It was a good job his fans were loyal because there were new writers coming through year after year and they all seemed to be able to publish books faster than he could.

The waiter brought the steak and he ate it with little relish. Whatever flavour had been in it to begin with had been driven out by about five minutes too long on the flames. At least the chips were tasty but it was hard to get them wrong, even if they did come straight out of the freezer.

He finished his third beer and took a last look outside. Rain dribbled down the window, making it impossible to see his reflection. He was pleased about that.

"Excuse me, Mr Night?" He'd heard the voice before, earlier today.

Ben turned and smiled. "Hello there." Seeing Fleur again made his smile a genuine one.

"I hope you don't mind me coming over. I waited until you'd finished eating."

She could have come over in the middle of his meal, it wouldn't have mattered. "No, of course not. Fleur, right?"

Her smile grew wider. "Oh wow, you remembered my name."

"I thought it was a nice name. I haven't heard it used very often."

There was an awkward silence as he waited for her to say what it was she wanted. It hadn't escaped his attention that she had changed clothes from their meeting earlier. She was wearing a dress that hugged her body. All of it.

"What can I do for you?" he asked.

She sat down without waiting to be invited. "I was wondering if you might spare me some tips?"

"Tips?"

"You know, for my writing." She moved her blonde hair off her shoulders with a flick of her head.

Rachel had been blonde too. He was a sucker for blondes. "Well, I'm not sure…"

"I'll buy you another one of those." She tapped the side of his bottle with her fingernail.

"There's no need to do that." He signalled to the waiter. "I'll have another please. And…?"

"A prosecco, please. If that's okay?" Fleur said without looking up.

"How many books have you written?" he asked. How

long had it been since he'd had a drink with a woman?

"Two and I'm part-way through another. It's hard fitting it around my job."

"Well, that's my first tip. Keep writing, keep getting those stories down and keep getting better. I wrote twelve before Howl was published. That's a lot of words and in those days…" He paused. Did he really want to start saying things like that, at a time like this? "It's easier now with computers."

The drinks arrived, quickly followed by another round. Before long the table was littered with empty beer bottles and Ben had a bad case of verbal diarrhoea. He knew he had but Fleur just sat there and listened. She seemed to be hanging on his every word. And the more he drank, the more he wondered what she looked like under the dress.

He knew that was the time to wind things up. He didn't want to get in a mess again, not after his previous form.

He drained the dregs from the bottle. "Listen, Fleur. I'm sorry but I have to be away early in the morning and it's already way past my bedtime. Do you need a taxi somewhere?" He looked for the waiter.

"No, I don't need one."

She had drunk four glasses of prosecco during the last couple of hours but looked sober enough.

"Driving?"

"Nope." She smiled and shook her head. "I'm staying here."

"Ah right, of course." He offered his hand. "I hope I've not waffled on too much and at least some of what I said makes sense. It was nice talking to you, Fleur."

She took his hand. "All of it made sense. I'll walk with you if that's okay?"

Ben stood up. "Okay"

They walked to the lift which was open as they reached it. He pressed the number six. He always requested the top floor. He couldn't stand to be disturbed by people stamping their feet in the room above.

"What number?" he asked.

"I'm coming to your room." Fleur took his hand.

He turned and looked at her. For a moment he was confused about what she meant but then it dawned on him.

"Are you sure?" he asked and regretted it immediately. What in god's name was he saying?

She kissed him on the lips. "Quite sure."

*

Ben woke in a confused daze. His eyes felt like they were glued shut. Not that he wanted to open them anyway. The light filtering through his eyelids was more than sufficient for the moment. He took a couple of deep breaths and licked his lips. They tasted of lipstick. It was a reminder, if he needed one, of Fleur.

He rolled onto his back and reached across the bed. It was empty and cold. Cold enough to have been vacant for some time. He had no recollection of her leaving, but then again the mini-bar had taken some hammering.

He risked it and opened his eyes. It wasn't as bad he thought but it was enough to send a stab of pain into the back of his head. He groaned, rolled over and swiped a finger across the screen of his phone. It was gone nine o'clock and he'd wanted to be long gone by now. He would have been too if he hadn't drunk too much and ended up in his room with a girl young enough to be his daughter. What an idiot.

He rolled out of bed and walked into the bathroom. The mirror was enormous, making it difficult to ignore his reflection as he climbed into the shower. The steam rose around him and he smiled. He wasn't married any more so it was nobody's business but his own who he slept with. Besides, it wasn't as if he'd gone out looking for someone. Fleur had come on to him, not the other way around. No, it was his business and that's exactly how it should stay. And she had been so… so… *firm*.

Breakfast was hard to stomach but he forced a croissant down with some strong coffee. He chose a table on the other side of the room to the one he'd sat at with Fleur. It was closer to the toilet in case breakfast didn't agree with him. He didn't know whether to cringe or grin as last night's activities came back to him. He'd done things that a middle-aged man shouldn't be doing. Not unless you were a rock star anyway.

Back in his room, he packed his belongings and made one last cup of instant coffee to get his brain working. As he drank it, he switched on his netbook and watched the news. Someone had killed a clown. Not just killed him but cut his face off and taken it away. There were some sick people out there. He sipped the coffee and burned his lips. Even the sugar he'd laced it with couldn't hide the bitterness.

"The victim, Harvey Newman, was also known by his working name of Bingo The Clown."

Ben turned the volume up. The screen showed a photograph of Bingo smiling at the camera. He reminded Ben of Sparkles. The dagger-like black diamonds around his eyes gave him the same appearance as the clown on the cover of Clownz. Who would do that? Who in their right mind would base their image on the cover of a monster clown in his book? Clownz hadn't been a bestseller by any means, but surely someone should have told the guy it was a bad look for a kids' show.

The reporter mumbled about connections to the occult but Ben was distracted by what was going on in the background. Police tape was stretched across the street and the white-suited forensic team were bringing out computer after computer from the address. Newman was obviously into his tech. As the camera panned across to the house, an officer was struggling with an enormous cardboard box in the doorway. He bumped it against the doorframe twice before he finally lost control and the contents spilled out.

There was a collection of brightly coloured wigs, some silly shoes and a variety of costumes in the box, and they all tumbled out in an untidy pile. A nose as red as a ruby bounced down the path like a ping-pong ball, leaving dirty red spots on the grey concrete path.

Ben leaned closer to the screen. "Shit," he whispered and rubbed his eyes. It had gone. The blood and the nose were both gone in an instant. He rubbed his eyes again and stretched his facial muscles. This was one of the worst hangovers in history.

The news flipped to another story about finance and he turned away. He wanted to check his emails before he left. He was waiting to hear back from his agent about a potential film deal for one of his monster books, Howl. He didn't want them turning the beast into a family-friendly, wronged and misunderstood werewolf. He was lots of things but friendly he most certainly wasn't. A healthy deal on film rights would save him in more ways than one.

There were no emails but there was some activity on his Twitter account, lots of activity in fact. He scrolled down the messages which were of a disconcertingly ambiguous nature. He could feel a sense of dread building in his guts.

He clicked on a link from a fan which read, 'Good to see a different side to Nightmare! LOL.'

Nightmare was his username and members of his fan club were called *Nightmares*. The first photograph showed him asleep in bed. His mouth was slightly ajar and he looked terrible. Not as terrible as the second photograph though. He was lying on his front with the sheets dripping off him. They had fallen so far that his arse cheeks were clearly on show for the world to see.

"Oh god." He lowered the screen. There were two others but he'd seen enough.

He drove home feeling irritated by the whole thing. Irritated and angry. He should have known better than that. Why would a girl who looked like Fleur be interested in him if it wasn't to get something out of it for herself? She'd get five minutes of fame with her followers and maybe some time with one of the tabloids, but he was hardly what anyone would call 'A' list. What was he? 'C' list or maybe even 'D' list these days. It was more likely that he had fallen off the list completely. He was at the bottom with the dead flies.

His phone kept ringing too. He could see who it was but wasn't going to answer it because he knew she would be mad. It was Joanne, his agent, and this was the sort of thing that made her blood boil. Would it harm the potential film deal? God, he hoped not.

She would keep ringing though. Ringing, ringing, ringing. That was her tactic – to wear you down, ring you into submission. It was making his head hurt worse than it already did.

He reached over to silence the phone and accepted the call by accident.

"Have you seen the charts?" she shouted.

"What? No." He felt a mixture of relief and confusion.

"You've got three books in the top twenty and Clownz is at three. It's gone crazy."

Ben took a moment to digest the information. "The horror chart?"

"No you tit, *the* chart. The entire chart. I'm looking for the link now but it looks like someone connected Clownz to that murder." She drew breath. "Tell me you've at least seen the news?"

"Yeah, yeah. Some clown got his face cut off. I'm not…"

"A clown called Bingo," she interrupted. "He looks just like the art on the first edition cover. Can you believe it? Who would do that?"

"Someone who hasn't read the book maybe?"

"Well, it doesn't matter. Just keep your nose clean and we'll get extra for the film rights."

He cringed and opened his mouth to say something but Joanne spoke before he had chance.

"Ah, here it is. One of the reporters was obviously a fan, he held your book up to the camera. It's an old edition by the looks of it. Why did we change the cover? That one's disturbing."

"Your idea, Jo. I always liked the first one." He could hear her tapping away on the computer.

"We'll change it back, I think. Leave it with me. I'll send you the film details when I get them. Bye."

And she was gone. Even if he had wanted to talk to her about the photographs of his naked bum, he couldn't get a word in edgeways. He'd talk to her tomorrow, when the hangover had subsided.

Three books in the top twenty, though. That had never happened before. Top one hundred a few times, but top twenty? Never.

It was a day of mixed news but all he wanted to do now was climb into bed and sleep. He pushed down harder on the pedal and accelerated into the rain.

3

Maldon stayed in bed for most of the next two days. He had only felt quite so ill once before, when he went cold turkey from heroin. He slept, he dreamt and his pores opened in a great gushing stream of rancid sweat. He remembered getting up twice to use the toilet but couldn't recall eating anything.

He stared up at the cobwebs on the ceiling and listened to his stomach rumble and gurgle. He'd been dreaming about his parents again. For years afterwards, he'd dreamt about the night they were killed. About the blood on the walls, on the carpet and on his skin. And for a while he'd been able to see their faces, particularly his mum's face just as the knife passed across her throat. She'd looked shocked but not in pain. Like someone had just played a bad trick on her.

Had killing Bingo been part of the dream too?

His pillow felt like a sponge and his legs were stuck to the sheets. The sour stench of stale body odour was everywhere, making his arid mouth feel drier by the second. He needed to get up, he needed to get out of bed and shower himself before he retched.

"Up and at 'em, Mouldy, jobs to do, people to see. Bingo's dead. Long live Sparkles!" A squeaky voice yelled from inside the holdall.

"Shut up!" Maldon shouted and climbed out of bed. The clown had been jabbering constantly for the last two days; telling jokes, being unkind and generally being a nuisance.

He walked to the bathroom, stepping over his copy of Clownz on the way. Had he left it in the middle of the room like that? He must have done but he didn't remember doing it. He climbed into the shower and started whistling the clown music. It made him feel better.

Cutting Bingo's face off had been an inspired idea. The clown had deprived him of a childhood. He had stolen Maldon's smile, his laughter, his parents. What better way to kill him than that? He wasn't entirely sure yet whether the resulting birth of Sparkles was a good thing or not.

He dried himself and walked back to the bedroom. The book was still on the floor, in the middle of the room. Where he had absolutely not left it.

"Pick it up, Maldon. Read it to me."

He looked at the bag and then at the book.

"Take me out and read me a story?" His voice was reedy and metallic. It sounded like it was coming through a voice changer, or belonged to a highly-strung cartoon character.

He crouched and opened the bag.

"Boo! Did I make you jump?" Sparkles had blood around

the corners of his mouth and where his eyes should have been. There was no mistaking him; the ghostly white face with black diamonds painted around his eyes. His smile was different though. It was smaller and it didn't turn up at the edges. There was no sense of happiness to it. In many ways it was just like his own non-existent smile.

He lifted the clown's face out of the bag. He had hoped his own smile would have come back by now. It had been two days and there was still no sign of it. His face looked and felt exactly the same as always.

"Where is your smile? Why are you not dancing and laughing like a lunatic? It looks like you didn't quite get what you wanted, Mouldy. Bingo wasn't the right man for you it seems. How very sad."

Maldon lifted Sparkles above his head. He wanted to hurl him at the wall. He wanted to hear the squelch as the face slapped into the dirty plaster. Sparkles would be just another stain.

"Want it back? Want smiles and laughter and jokes and all manner of fun and games?" Sparkles's voice went up another octave.

Maldon paused. That was exactly what he wanted. What he had yearned for, for as long as he could remember.

"I can give it to you. This time next week you'll be laughing like a drain, Mouldy. You'll be singing and dancing and I'll transform that ugly downturned mouth of yours into a radiant thing of beauty. How does that grab you?"

Maldon nodded but didn't make a sound.

"Look at that book down there. Look at my smile!"

Maldon looked down at Clownz, at the startling and vivid cover.

"We want the same thing. We both want to smile again."

Maldon opened his mouth to object but closed it again. Clowns knew more about laughter and smiling than anyone else. His own plan hadn't worked, he remained utterly miserable.

"Come on, whaddaya say? I'll bring the music?"

Immediately Maldon's beloved circus music started up inside his head. It was called Entry of the Gladiators, he knew that because he'd looked it up several years ago. It was scratchy, faint and a little out of tune but it was there again and it was wonderful. He sat down cross-legged beside the book and put Sparkles face up on his knee.

"Where do we start?"

"You know where, you just need a gentle shove in the right direction. We'll need the knife. Now are you going to read to me? I can't do it myself, I ain't got no peepers."

Maldon picked up the book and turned to the first chapter. He started reading but he could have recited the opening two chapters from memory.

"The circus was here! Multicoloured posters of clowns and fire-breathers and lion tamers decorated every single wall in the town. And if the children stood close enough to the pictures, the smell of candyfloss and hot dogs drifted down into their cute little nostrils. 'Can we go, Mum?' they asked. 'Can we go and see the clowns?'

"The mums and dads, they all agreed of course. But had they looked close enough at the clown on the poster, they would have seen something different to the children. Underneath the cheerful mask, the clown sneered and whispered with rancid breath into their ears, 'Boo!'

"Sparkles was…"

"Boring, boring, boring! Yawn, yawn, yawn! Is that the best you can do?" Sparkles interrupted.

Maldon was shocked. "What? It's… it's…"

"Unoriginal. That's what it is. Now what say we make our own story? It'll be better than this codswallop and totally original."

"I wouldn't know where to begin."

"Nonsense," Sparkles replied. *"I'll help you."*

"And what will it be about?" Maldon asked.

"Me, of course! What else?"

Maldon nodded. It was the obvious choice, "We'll need a title too."

"That we will, that we will. Hmm, Sparkles the Second?"

"Boo!" Maldon said.

"Perfect!" Sparkles squealed.

Maldon carried Sparkles downstairs and sat at the kitchen table. He put him down very carefully and started the computer. It was old and slow and took an age to start up, but it was fine for looking at porn. When it finally started, the wallpaper was a never-ending carousel of all the front covers for Clownz. His favourite had always been the edition he'd read in prison. It was the first edition.

"You know, Maldon, it's awfully dark in here, can we put a light on? I can't see properly."

"The light is on," Maldon replied.

"Oh! Hmm, would you be willing to hold me up a touch? Just a smidgen closer to the light? I'll be able to help you more if I can see. Turn me so I can see the screen."

Maldon lifted him.

"Higher," Sparkles whispered.

Maldon lifted him until he was in front of his face.

"That's better. Now a teensy-weensy bit closer to you."

Maldon did as he was asked.

"Closer," he whispered.

"I can't get any closer." Maldon was starting to feel irritated by the demands. Sparkles was almost touching his own face.

"Oh yes you can!"

And then Sparkles was on his face. Clinging to it like a lump of raw meat. Only Sparkles wasn't cold and he didn't feel wet or uncomfortable. He felt snug and… and, well… a perfect fit.

"There, that's much better. I can see properly now. Can you hear my music? Just listen to it, is it not just the most beautiful music in the whole world!"

"It's called Entry of the Gladiators," Maldon stated.

"Indeed it is, Maldon. Indeed it is. Now, let us begin our masterpiece!"

*

Jane Brady was tired. Dog tired. She'd been awake for twenty hours straight and every time she looked at the computer screen, an electric shock passed through her eyeballs and into her brain. She wasn't going to be useful for much longer.

The search team had found eleven computers at Newman's house. Eleven computers. Then there were a further three in bits in the garage and four external hard drives. The man could have been a computer geek. He could even have been building them as a sideline to his 'Bingo The Clown' kids' party business. But something told her this wasn't the case. Twenty-four years of being a police officer told her there was something nasty about it.

"What's on the report, Sarge?" DC Stu Kelly was the only other officer in the incident room. He'd been lazy when he mentored her ten years ago. Jane had gone up a rank since then but Kelly had remained a DC. He only had a couple of years left to go before he got his pension and he wasn't pulling up any trees, that was for sure.

She stared at him for a moment. "Shouldn't you be at home?"

He shrugged. "I've been home and come back. It's you who needs to go home, Jane."

She looked away. Just like Kelly to look after himself. There were ten other officers including herself who hadn't been home, yet somehow Kelly had found the time to slope off for a few hours. She picked up the phone and started ringing around the team. They were all out on enquiries but the urgent ones had all been completed now. There was nothing more to be done tonight and she needed them to be fit for another long day tomorrow.

"Does that mean I can get an early one too?" Kelly asked.

Jane fixed him with a stare again and he smirked. "Can't blame me for trying." He put his head back down and shuffled some paperwork.

She would go soon too, get four or five hours kip and then be back for morning briefing. First she had to look at the report, though. She'd been putting it off for the last twenty minutes. She wasn't sure if her eyes or her brain could stomach what she thought was coming next.

The High-Tech Crime Unit had fast-tracked the computers but it would take days, possibly weeks, for them to work through Newman's entire stash. Nevertheless a preliminary report had been completed on the first computer, the one in his bedroom. The one with clown stickers all down the side of the monitor. The mouse mat was a picture of him and beneath his picture was the caption, 'Bingo The Clown – Tickling Ribs since 1982!'

"I hate clowns," she whispered and clicked on the email with the HTCU report attached.

There were thirty pages in all and twenty-five of them detailed the most horrific filth imaginable. The other pages were filled with the legal powers the author had used to examine the computer. Over two hundred category-five images, the worst possible, and thousands of others on this computer alone.

After the first page, she didn't need to see any more. Not tonight anyway.

"Vigilante?" Kelly was peering over her shoulder.

"Have you been at the raw garlic again, Stu?" She could see his big, red drinker's nose out of the corner of her eye. It was revolting.

He moved back. "Sorry, spag bol."

"Glad you've had time to eat something. Possibility,

there's some kid's party photos in there. Someone's going to have to go through all these and try to see if we've got any identifiable victims." She noticed Kelly was already walking away, trying to distance himself from any work that might be coming his way. He was safe though, she wouldn't want him within a thousand miles of anything requiring a sensitive hand.

The phone rang and she snatched at it. "DS Brady, incident room."

She waited for the operator in the call centre to finish completely before replying. She was making decisions while taking in the information.

"Okay, we schedule it for…" She checked her watch. "Four hours time. That's 7am when the child abuse DS comes on duty. At the same time I want it scheduling for DI White and DCI Hargreaves, I'll brief them both. Can you type something on the incident please? I'll dictate it." She waited a moment and then continued.

"I have reviewed the information available at this time. These are allegations of historical abuse where the victim is now an adult. There are no forensic matters to consider at this time. As a result I request this incident be scheduled for the Child Abuse Investigation Unit and Divisional CID in the morning. I will be on duty to brief DI White. Please link to Operation Mint. DS Brady."

She ended the call and rubbed her eyes with the heels of her palms. It sent a spike of pain through her skull.

"It doesn't look like we'll need to look very far for his victims," she said to herself.

"Oh?" Kelly was back at his desk.

"Nope, it looks like they're coming to us. I need to go and grab a couple of hours but I'm only going down to the First Aid Room. Just field the phones please, Stu."

Jane walked down the corridor. Two victims had phoned in, reporting abuse at Newman's hands. It was likely that the two would be multiplied many times over in the next few days, judging by what was on his computer. That investigation would be taken on by either Child Abuse or CID, probably both, but she wanted to keep at least some involvement in it. There were going to be links.

She'd seen some things in the last twenty-four years that made her toes curl, but never before had she seen someone with their face cut off like that. If it was one of his victims and they wanted to cut something off, why not his cock? That was the obvious place to start.

She climbed onto the treatment table and folded her jacket under her head. She might get a couple of hours if she was lucky. She set an alarm for three hours time and closed her eyes. She had a job for Kelly tomorrow. Good old 'Bingo' had five copies of the same paperback book in his wardrobe with a horrible clown face on the cover. All of them signed to him personally. The author needed speaking to.

She drifted into sleep and saw clowns in her dreams, riding bicycles that were several sizes too small. Even that looked creepy now.

*

Jane was back in the office before anyone else. Except for Stu Kelly who was fast asleep with his shoes on his desk and his mouth wide open.

"Morning, Stu!" she shouted across the room.

He opened his eyes and looked about the office, trying to remember where he was.

"Must've drifted off for a minute." He lowered his feet and stood up. "Tea?"

"Coffee, please. Strong coffee." She sat down at her desk and logged in. Kelly looked like he'd been asleep for more than just a minute or two. He had probably been asleep for the same amount of time as her. That was on top of the two or three hours he'd managed to sneak in yesterday.

She loaded her emails and stared at the screen. There were six missed calls, the last one only two minutes ago.

"Did anyone phone for me while I was gone?"

He turned and shook his head. "Not that I heard." He quickly turned back to the kettle.

"Says here I missed six calls."

Kelly just ignored the comment and stirred the cups. He was good at ignoring things.

Jane scrolled down the list. They were all from the call centre and all were linked to the historical abuse call she had taken earlier this morning.

"Looks like everyone's got up this morning and decided to phone us. We've got calls from all over the county."

Kelly put a cup of instant coffee down on the desk. "I was hoping to get away early tonight. I've been on since…"

She didn't let him finish. "This one's for you." She passed

him a sheet of paper. On it was an 'action' for him to go and talk to Ben Night, author of, amongst other books, Clownz. He needed to find out why Harvey Newman had so many copies of his book, all of them signed.

Kelly took it from her and stomped across the office. It might only take him a couple of hours and she might let him go home then anyway. It depended on how much sulking he did.

"Morning, Jane." DI White walked in, followed by the DCI. They both nodded at Kelly and walked straight into the White's office.

"Talk to me when you get back, Stu. I'm going to brief the boss." She walked toward the DI's office.

Kelly didn't look up. It looked like he was trying to smash his keyboard to bits.

4

Ben's throat had been on fire since spending the night with Fleur. It felt like someone had carved it up with a razor blade and then rubbed salt deep down into the cuts. Every swallow was like torture. Not only had she photographed his arse and splashed it across social media but she had given him a nasty throat infection. He shuddered to think what other infections she might have given him.

He stood in front of the bathroom mirror and opened his mouth. The culprits were clearly visible – little white blisters all over his throat.

"Bitch." He put his head into the sink and splashed cold water on his face. He felt like he had a fever too. That had come on in the night when he had woken up in a pool of sweat from some pretty vivid dreams. His head felt like someone had put it in a vice and was slowly tightening the screw.

He stood up, gripping the edge of the sink to stop himself falling back. It was of no comfort to see that he looked as bad as he felt. What he needed was to spend the day in bed. Possibly the next two days. Even if he had enough material to write something, there was no way he could get anything cohesive down, not today.

He shuffled out of the en-suite in his slippers and nothing else, and fell face-first onto the bed. It smelled of sweat but he didn't care. And if someone else wanted to come and photograph his bare backside, they were welcome to. He should probably contact that bitch and tell her what he thought of her.

He started to drift off but was disturbed by a knock on the front door.

"Piss off," he mumbled into the sheets.

The knocking came again, followed by the doorbell. It was a terrible tune, something to do with gladiators. Joanne, his agent, had sent it as a joke when Clownz first hit the semi-big-time. It was just irritating and seemed to go on forever. Why hadn't he dismantled it by now? Probably because nobody ever used it. Nobody ever came to the house.

He groaned and ignored it. Whoever it was would get the message soon enough. The knocking started again, followed by the doorbell.

"Shut up, shut up, shut up!" he shouted, wincing at the pain in his throat. He stumbled off the bed and walked to the window, forgetting he was naked.

There was a man down below. If his car hadn't been so crappy, Ben might have thought he was there to sell something. The man stepped back and looked up. He lifted a hand in greeting.

Ben lifted his own hand and was about to give him the finger when the man held up a badge. A policeman's badge.

"Two minutes," he mouthed through the window and the officer gave the thumbs-up in reply. Was giving a police officer the finger an offence? He looked down at his exposed genitals. Flashing one most certainly was.

What could they want with him? He'd driven back from the signing in a temper and had probably been speeding. No, not probably, definitely. Did they make house calls for speeding tickets?

"Nearly gave him an eyeful there, Stan," he croaked. The dog eyed him from the foot of the bed. Stan was a retired greyhound and he hated his routine being disturbed. His routine mainly consisted of sleeping, and sometimes even eating seemed a chore.

Ben dressed quickly, went downstairs and opened the front door. A cold wind blew in and he wished he'd put a sweatshirt on, not just a t-shirt.

"Hello?"

"Mr Night?" the man asked.

"That's right. What can I do for you?" Stan had managed to drag himself out of bed and was leaning against him with his teeth chattering in his usual excited fashion.

The officer held his badge and warrant card out for Ben to examine. "DC Kelly. Can I have a word, please?"

Ben stepped to the side. "Of course, come in."

Kelly smiled, picked up a briefcase and walked past him. He smelled of garlic and his shirt was stretched too tightly across his gut. The buttons looked like they might pop at any time. Stan wagged his tail and sniffed Kelly as he walked past but Kelly didn't acknowledge the dog in any way. When Stan saw this was not someone to get excited about, he slunk back upstairs for a lie down.

"Which way?" Kelly asked and pointed left and right.

Ben stepped around him and led him into the lounge. "Can I get you a drink, DC Kelly?" He suddenly felt very nervous.

"A coffee would be good. Milk and one sugar please."

"Give me a couple of minutes, I'll be right back."

"Don't go running out of the back door, will you!" Kelly laughed at his own joke.

Ben walked out of the lounge, across the hall into the kitchen-diner. The thought hadn't crossed his mind until now. Maybe it should have. He laughed but it sounded forced.

A few minutes later he came back into the room with two mugs. His was filled with hot lemon drink, which he hoped contained enough painkiller to stun his throat into a temporary submission.

Kelly was sitting on the sofa with his briefcase next to him. The sofa looked directly at the widescreen television on the wall. The only time Ben used the room was when he sprawled across the sofa to watch sports. Usually with a four-pack and a bowl of cheesy nachos.

He passed Kelly his coffee and sat in the armchair. "What is it you want to speak to me about?"

He nodded at Ben's drink. "Under the weather?"

"What? Yes, a bit of a sore throat."

"Too much kissing eh?" Kelly winked.

"Something like that. So…" He was getting impatient. He didn't get many social calls but an overweight copper with bad breath wouldn't be a first on his list of invites anyway.

"How do you know Harvey Newman?"

"Who?" Ben answered. He felt relieved. He had no idea who Harvey Newman was.

"Harvey Newman. The man who was murdered two days ago."

Ben frowned. He was still drawing a blank.

"Bingo. Does that ring a bell?" Kelly's voice had a trace of sarcasm in it.

Was he being a bit slow because of his temperature? All he could think of was Sparkles in Clownz, but it was ridiculous to be thinking about a fictional character when a police officer was asking him questions.

Kelly sighed, which irritated him, and then it came to him. He'd seen the reporter outside the address, and in the background they had been loading a van full of computers. Hadn't there been a red nose bouncing down the drive too, leaving blood spots on the floor? No, that was just his imagination.

"The guy who got his face cut off?" he asked. "Never met him." Why did they want to know that? Just because the victim was a clown and he had written a book about a clown didn't mean they automatically knew each other.

Kelly leaned over and opened his briefcase with a loud 'click'. His hand was out of Ben's view for a moment, then he withdrew it and handed a book to him. It was a first edition of Clownz with the original artwork on the cover.

"Open it at the front," Kelly said.

Ben looked at him and then at the book. "Who does it belong to?"

"Just open it, Mr Night."

Ben wanted to tell him to stop issuing orders and throw him out, but he wanted to know what was going on first. And there was the question of whether it was appropriate to throw a policeman out of your house. He opened the book and saw his handwriting. It was in slightly faded black ink but it was unmistakable.

The message said, *'To Harvey, keep reading and I'll keep writing!'* It was followed by his signature.

"Do you know how many books I've signed, DC Kelly? Hundreds, probably thousands. This could have been twenty years ago. Why do you expect me to remember this particular one?"

Kelly fished in his briefcase and handed another edition of Clownz to him.

"What about this?" He looked smug as if he'd caught Ben out somehow.

He took the book. It was another edition of Clownz, a later one with less lurid artwork on the cover. He opened it before he was told to. There was another inscription from him.

'To my biggest Nightmare, Harvey!'

He handed the books back to Kelly whose grin was growing by the second. Kelly put them on his knee.

"Are these evidence? Exhibits?" Ben asked.

Kelly took a sip of his coffee, licked his lips and replied, "Not yet."

"What does that mean?" The drink had taken the edge off his throat but his head was pounding, sending waves of pain into his eyes.

Kelly put the books in his case. "There are three more just like it. Do you want to see the others?" He paused and wiped a dribble of coffee from his lips. "It might refresh your memory?"

"Like I said, I sign hundreds of books every year, sometimes more. There's no way I'd remember one person out of all of those." Although he doubted he would forget Fleur in a hurry.

"You're sweating, Mr Night."

Ben wiped his brow. It felt cold and clammy. "It's just a temperature, that's all." He could feel Kelly scrutinising him. He hadn't done anything wrong and he didn't know this 'Harvey', but he was starting to feel like he was in trouble.

"Is that all it is?" Kelly asked.

"What? What exactly are you trying to say?" He was starting to lose his temper now.

Kelly closed his case. "Nothing, I was just asking…"

"Are you finished, because I need to go back to bed." He cut the detective off before he could spout any more rubbish.

"You're absolutely sure you don't know him?"

Ben stood up and felt dizziness wash over him. "I'm quite sure. Why he chose to paint his face that way is beyond me. I take it you haven't read Clownz?"

"Not my thing." Kelly finished his coffee, stood up and handed the cup to Ben.

"Well, let's just say Sparkles wasn't exactly a kid's best friend." He started walking toward the front door. Kelly followed behind.

"Neither was Harvey Newman, or his alter ego, Bingo The Clown." Kelly raised his eyebrows.

"He wasn't?"

"Watch the news, Mr Night."

Ben opened the door for him. "That's it then?"

Kelly walked away. "We'll be in touch."

Ben watched him waddle to his car. What would they be in touch about? There was nothing else to say. The wind whipped across the open fields and sent an icy chill into the house. As a powerful shiver rippled through his body, he grunted and slammed the door.

Kelly was an obnoxious man, regardless of his job. It was sad that a clown with an unfortunate name had been murdered but Ben didn't know him, no matter how many books he'd signed over the years. If someone had turned up to a book signing dressed as a clown he might remember, but even then, aside from Fleur he seldom had anything to do with any of them.

He walked back to the lounge and turned the television on. It took him a while to find the news channel, but once he did he could see exactly what Kelly meant about Newman not being a friend to children.

"Police have confirmed today that there have been a number of reports of abuse at the hands of murdered clown

Harvey Newman. The cases are believed to stretch back over some thirty years. Police are attempting to identify further victims and are urging people to come forward if they have ever booked Newman, who worked under the name 'Bingo The Clown', to appear at any events. Newman was..."

Ben switched it off. He felt sick. Very, very sick. He had shaken hands with Newman on at least five occasions. What had those hands done? He closed his eyes and felt the room revolve around him. Had Newman got his sick inspiration from him? Had he based his own actions on those of the fictional clown? It was vile. The fictional Sparkles had eaten kids' brains, he hadn't... he hadn't...

Was the room spinning faster? He needed to go and lie down upstairs. He needed to sleep and to forget about Harvey Newman and Sparkles.

He put his hands on the wall and used it to balance and guide himself up the stairs. His legs felt like jelly as he collapsed onto the bed. John Wayne Gacy had been the inspiration, or at least he'd provided the idea, for a killer clown in Clownz. Gacy, the notorious American serial killer, had slaughtered at least thirty-three people but he also had an alter ego. He donned the facade of Pogo the Clown to entertain people in his home town. Nobody suspected what was truly behind the mask. Art imitating life. And now his book had been used as the inspiration for a deranged paedophile to get access to children. Life imitating art, full circle complete. It was appalling and horrific.

He closed his eyes and felt the room turn in a nauseating circle. Tomorrow he would rip the door chime off the wall and smash it to bits. Every copy of Clownz he owned would be hidden away. Joanne said it was in the top ten but he didn't want anyone else to read it. He'd think about getting the publisher to pull it from the shelves. At least until all this died down. It was distasteful, at the very least. All of his money had gone, all his ideas were withered and cliché and Fleur had seen to his self-respect, but none of that mattered beside the atrocities inflicted on the children by that clown. He slipped into a fevered sleep.

*

Ben had no idea what time it was, nor did he care. His entire body felt like it was on fire, literally being burned alive from the inside. He groaned and brought his hands to his face. It was covered in sweat, sticky and cold. He couldn't stand to open his eyes but could tell it was dark. He wished he'd been clever enough to put a glass of water beside the bed earlier.

He had been dreaming about Sparkles. There had been some kind of circus in town. It had a huge red and white striped big top filled with clowns eating people's brains, and in the background, a band of clowns was playing the terrible carnival music on instruments made of bones. The music was badly out of tune.

His head was still spinning, his thoughts random and fleeting. He knew he was in some kind of confused delirium and that sleep was the only way out of the other side. He rolled over onto his side, opening his eyes for a moment.

"Hi, Sparkles." He tried to lift his arm to wave but he was too weak. Sparkles was standing in the doorway to his room, just standing there staring at him. The sound of Stan's chattering teeth was like bones rattling together, so loud it hurt his ears.

"Don't get excited, Stan, it's just a dream. You're not going to eat my brain are you, Sparkles?" He laughed but the clown was being miserable tonight. He looked a bit sorry for himself. He looked a mess. His make-up was all over the place and his big, red bulbous nose was missing. It was red though, red and kind of gruesome looking. And what about his costume? Sparkles never wore grubby brown overalls. Oh well, maybe he was ill too.

"Night night." He smiled, closed his eyes and listened to the clown's footsteps on the stairs.

*

His bladder woke him up with a level of pain that said if he didn't haul himself out of bed in the next two minutes, not only would he be lying in sweat, he would also be lying in urine. At some point, he had managed to strip down to his boxer shorts but the night had been a confused mishmash of dreams and reality.

As soon as he moved, Stan was up on his feet and round to the side of the bed. The dog pushed his nose under the duvet and nudged at Ben's hand.

"Need to go out do you, boy?" His voice sounded like someone else's. He reached out and stroked the dog's wonderfully soft head. Stan moved so Ben could scratch him behind the ear. His teeth chattered and it made his lower jaw vibrate in a blur.

"Give me two minutes and I'll get you breakfast and then you can go kill some more grass."

Stan cocked his head and wagged his tail. He didn't understand many words but 'breakfast' was one of them.

Ben swung his legs over the side of the bed and grunted. His entire body felt like he had been in a car crash, one where the car finished upside down on its roof. He took four steps and felt the room slide to the left. He took two more and grabbed the bathroom's door frame to steady himself. It was like being in a funhouse at the fair. Too bad it wasn't in the slightest bit funny.

After he had finished on the toilet, he filled the sink with cold water and submerged his face. The odour of stale sweat drifted off him like a noxious cloud. He knew he should shower but the thought of jets of water smashing onto his body made him feel sick. He sucked some water into his mouth and squeezed it down his throat. The pain was immediate and intense, and it made one of his legs buckle at the knee. It was a good job he was gripping the edge of the sink.

What did they say about bad throats? Something about eating toast to scratch the blisters of pus away, wasn't it?

He pulled his dressing gown off the back of the door and walked slowly downstairs. Every few steps, the world skewed to one side then the other. This wasn't just a sore throat, this was a full-blown case of flu.

Eating the toast was arduous, painful and slow. Each piece became tree bark in the length of time it took him to force it down. He finished it and looked out from the kitchen to the fields. The view was almost to the horizon but it was a desolate and barren vista at this time of year. In the spring months, the fields glowed with flowering rape. It was a short but vivid display.

Stan was slinking his way around the edge of the field with his nose to the ground. He paused, lifted his head to sniff the air, then put his head back down and continued his trail. The dog once belonged to Rachel. She had listened to a programme on the radio about what they did to retired racing dogs and immediately declared that she wanted not one, but two. And that was that.

Dolly had always hovered wherever Rachel was, whimpering and hopping around nervously if they weren't together, whereas Stan mostly just slept and accepted affection from whoever offered it. When he went outside and there were rabbits close by, he would wag his tail, chatter his teeth at them and then get down to the serious business of sniffing. At twelve years old, his hunting and sprinting days were behind him but Ben suspected the chattering of teeth carried a little bit of menace, to the rabbits at least.

When Rachel left, she took Dolly but not Stan. Stan didn't seem bothered about it. Ben suspected that Dolly's constant state of anxiety and nervous whimpering irritated him and kept him from sleeping as much as he'd like. On the rare occasion that Stan was exercised at a park, he would avoid other dogs like the plague. He would hide behind trees, bushes and buildings, and if any dogs came near him he would put the pedal down and break into a jog. With his long legs, his jog was too fast for most other dogs. He was, by and large, antisocial which suited Ben down to the ground.

Living in the middle of nowhere had its benefits – not many unwanted callers, for one – but on rare occasions he found himself wishing he could walk to a pub with Stan and have a drink. As long as nobody bothered him, it would be fine. Even when Rachel suggested it, they took it in turns to drive so the other one could have a drink. Not that they went very often. How long had Rachel been gone now? Nearly two years. Wasn't that the same amount of time since he'd written anything even half-decent? He knew that wasn't a coincidence.

He looked awful. His reflection at the hotel had been bad but this, well this took the prize. He looked almost as bad as… as bad as the clown had looked, last night. The clown who stood at his bedroom door and stared at him, watching him sleep.

He shivered and turned away. That had just been a dream, a trick his fevered mind had conjured up to taunt him about Harvey Newman. That reminded him. If he did one thing today, it would be to remove the battery from the door chime. Just thinking about that tune made his skin crawl.

His office was a small room off the kitchen, and as well as housing his computer, it also contained his tool box. Not that he was any good at DIY, he wasn't, he was utterly useless but he liked to have a tool box. It made him feel more *manly*.

The kettle boiled and he made himself a Lemsip. He carried it through to the office with both hands wrapped around the mug, using his aching backside to open the door. He stepped through and looked at his computer.

The mug fell from his hands and smashed on the tiled floor. He barely noticed the scalding liquid burning his toes as he stared at what was on the keyboard.

5

Stu Kelly sat in the briefing and stared at the clock. It was already an hour past his finish time, and by the time this pointless exercise was finished it would be close to two hours. He chewed his pen and sighed. Some of these wet-behind-the-ears detectives couldn't get enough of it. They would be happy to stay all night if they were asked. Wait until they had been at this game for nearly thirty years, let's see how enthusiastic they were then.

He looked to the front of the room. Brady was trying to motivate them all, now they knew Newman was a dirty kiddie-fiddler. In his opinion, not that it counted for much, old 'Bingo' got exactly what he deserved.

It had to be said, Brady had a good pair on her. He spent a lot of time considering her tits when they worked together; a lot of time thinking about what they might look like under her neatly pressed blouses.

"Are you with us, Stu?" Brady asked.

"What? Sorry." He heard a few sniggers in the room.

"I was just saying, I'd like you to go through the CCTV footage again."

He screwed his face up. "What? Again? I went through it yesterday."

"Yes, Stu. As I said, we now have a better idea of the times so I want you to concentrate on a specific frame of reference."

He sighed, very loud. He wanted her to know how he felt about it. "No problem."

They stared at each other for a moment and the room was silent. He knew she wanted to have a go at him but she wouldn't do that in front of everyone. He'd slip out after the briefing before she had chance.

The clock ticked on and Brady droned on. Finally, she asked for questions, which thankfully none of them had. He closed his book, which might have to be disposed of before it entered the evidential chain. The pictures of Jane Brady's breasts might not go down well with a judge.

"Stu, can I have a word, please?"

His heart sank. This would be another ten minutes of his life he wouldn't get back. The room emptied and he walked to Brady.

She looked pissed off. "Stu, at least try to pretend you're interested. You can't behave like that."

"I'm sorry, I'm just tired." He wasn't particularly, he just wanted to get home and have a drink.

"We all are. Just try. Okay?"

He nodded and smiled. "Okay if I go now?"

Brady nodded. "See you at seven."

He turned and walked away. As soon as he pushed through the doors he mouthed the word 'bitch'.

*

Kelly thought about Brady as he drove home. He hated her. She had a big mouth and she thought she knew better than everyone else. He knew what she was up to. She was giving him all the crappy jobs that nobody else wanted. First she had him driving to the middle of nowhere to talk to some writer. He clearly hadn't got a clue what was happening, in fact he looked half-dead. Then she had him on a CCTV trawl and that made him late home yesterday. Late for the match, late for his kebab and late for his beer. Now he was late home tonight as well. DS Brady, what a joke.

Bitch. She was the reason he'd been sidelined for promotion too. That incident with the prostitute had nearly got him the sack. She had dropped him right in it. From a great height. They dangled his balls over the fire for a whole year over that one. They were all bitches. Know-it-all bitches who thought they were better than him.

Kelly pulled onto his driveway and switched off the engine. On his last day, he was going to tell her exactly what he thought of her. He was going to tell a lot of people what he thought about them. That day couldn't come soon enough, but he had to keep his nose clean for the next couple of years so he could get his hands on that juicy pension. Mary would have to get her share, of course. She was a bitch too. An ex-wife bitch.

He leaned over and picked up the bags from the

passenger seat. One had his dinner in. Chicken bhuna, pillau rice, peshwari naan and a bag of chips on the side. It would probably give him a nasty case of indigestion all night and bad guts in the morning but it was worth it. The other bag had eight cans of lager in. It was buy one get one half-price, so it seemed a shame not to take them up on the offer.

He hauled himself out of the car with a grunt. If he could make it through the next two years and avoid doing the fitness test, he would be a very happy man. He got inside and closed the door. One thing he should be grateful for was that he wasn't involved in the child abuse case. That looked like it might be a long and difficult job and had the potential to get messy. No, if Kelly was lucky, the bosses would send him back to divisional CID where he knew how to avoid work. He'd perfected it over the last ten years.

He walked into the kitchen and put his bags on the worktop. It felt chilly tonight, he might have to put the heating on. He pulled a can out of the bag, opened it and took a long drink. That was better. Almost immediately he could feel the alcohol taking the edge off his day.

Kelly shivered. It really was cold, almost as if there was a breeze blowing through the house. He could hear cars on the main road. He couldn't usually hear them unless there was a window open. He looked up. The small window at the top of the double-glazed unit was open. He stood on tiptoes and reached up, his gut bumping against the sink. No, it wasn't open exactly. The entire pane of glass was missing. Just gone.

Burglars.

That was his first thought. It was as simple as removing

the beading from around the frame and lifting the glass out.

He peered into the back garden. It was dark out there, except for a wedge of light shining onto the grass from next door's conservatory. He could feel his heart beating faster. Faster and louder. There was a chance they were still in the house. Good. In all his years, he'd never caught a burgling shit in the act. Reasonable and appropriate force, that was what the law said about detaining a criminal. Well, tonight that force may turn out to be unreasonable, particularly if the little shit struggled.

Hold on. What was that down by the shed? Movement, slow and deliberate movement. And now someone was standing like a statue staring up at him. Someone with a face that looked too white. So pale, in fact, that it might belong to one of the corpses he'd found during his career.

Only it was too close. So close that he could see it wasn't a corpse or a mannequin, it was a clown. An ugly distorted clown with a ragged, bloody line around the contours of his face.

It was behind him. The clown was in the kitchen behind him.

A cold shiver crept up the back of Kelly's neck and his heart hammered with a power and speed that boomed in his ears.

"Boo!" the clown whispered into his ear.

*

Jane gathered the paperwork together in a neat pile and pushed it into a folder. She was going with the DI to brief the Superintendent on the progress of the investigation. Her paperwork was all in order, she knew what her team were up to and the state of all of their enquiries. Nevertheless, she was still nervous. She always was when she briefed someone that far up the rankings, despite having done it on at least ten other major investigations.

She walked across the office. It was full of detectives either on the phone or tapping away at computers.

"Anyone seen Stu yet?" His desk was empty.

A voice shouted "He's probably still pissed." A few sniggers went around the room.

She walked out and up the corridor. It was a possibility. His last manager had given Stu a breath test when he came on duty, such was the smell of booze on him. He'd passed, somehow, but it was well known that Stu Kelly was an alcoholic.

If he hadn't turned up by the time she finished the briefing, she would go to his house and give him a warning. It wasn't time for him to see the boss, and she hoped it wouldn't come to that, but he needed to think about his pension, if nothing else.

She straightened her jacket and knocked on the Superintendent's door. She could do without babysitting Stu on top of everything else.

A little later, she came out of the briefing feeling a lot better than when she went in. DI White took most of the credit for how well the investigation was going, but he'd at least passed some of that down the chain to her. The Super was giving a press conference later that afternoon so he wanted to be fully appraised. It was satisfying to be able to answer all of his questions without once having to look in her book. Jane knew from experience that it gave him enormous confidence to see that in his officers.

She left the DI with him and walked back to the office. It was quieter now and only two officers were still at their desks. They were both on the phone but there was no sign of Stu. She hoped he had been in and was already at the CCTV suite going back over the footage.

She opened her emails, seeing there was another report from the computer geeks. She didn't envy them their job. Going through thousands of vile images, categorising them and then going home to their families as if it were just another day.

One of the detectives put his phone down. "Has Stu gone out already?" she asked him.

"I haven't seen him. What about you, Griff?" He looked over his monitor at the officer on the other side who held a phone to his ear, clearly on hold.

"Nope, he hasn't appeared yet."

Jane's heart sank. She picked up her mobile and found him in the contacts.

"Pick up, pick up," she whispered as it rang but there was no answer.

She ended the call and drummed her fingers on the desk. She was tired, they all were. Living on chocolate, coffee, and salt and vinegar crisps wasn't something you could do forever. Not and stay alert and capable, anyway. Stu was taking the piss like he always did, and she'd had enough of it.

She slung her harness around her shoulders and slipped her jacket on over the top.

"I'm going out for a bit. If you need me, I'm on my mobile." She stomped out of the office.

Stu had probably been a decent officer at some point in his career but what she knew of him wasn't good. He was lazy, arrogant, rude and disrespectful. The incident with the prostitute was her first real picture of him.

He was her mentor, a senior detective in the division, and they had been sent to deal with an allegation of rape by a street worker.

The girl had been hysterical, her make-up was smudged and her clothes ripped and dirty. She had shrieked and wailed, and it took ten minutes in the back of the car to calm her down. When she was composed enough to speak, Stu had spent as much time talking her out of making a complaint as it would have taken to actually start the investigation.

"Who's going to believe you were raped? Who's going to believe a prostitute? You're better off forgetting about it."

But she had insisted and he took her back to the police station. He had deliberately kept Jane out of the room while he spoke to her and sent her off on some ridiculous errand. When she came back Stu was smiling, as if he had just single-handedly solved a murder.

"She made it up. I'll write the report," he said. Jane hadn't yet grown the confidence to challenge him. The girl had complained about both of them, and although she wouldn't report the rape for fear of not being taken seriously, they had both ended up in trouble.

Being summoned to Professional Standards was an unwelcome episode in her career, but she had been given no choice in providing a full explanation about how they dealt with the initial complaint. Stu was suspended and she got management advice, which she was still deeply ashamed about.

She pulled up on the road outside his house. If he was drunk inside the house, she would have no choice but to inform DI White. She didn't want Stu to lose his pension but he needed a massive wake-up call.

The front garden was unkempt and the windows looked like they could do with a clean. She had been here once before, when Stu's suspension was lifted. He held a party but god alone knew why he'd invited her. His wife had given Jane some cold stares that evening. She was long gone by now.

She knocked on the front door and peered in through the window. There was nothing out of place and no sign of an overweight drunkard with a bulbous nose lying comatose and dribbling in the armchair.

She opened the letter box and shouted, "Stu, it's Jane, can you let me in, please?"

She cocked her head and listened for any noise. The house was silent so she called again.

"Come on, Stu, come and open the door."

She took her phone out, pressed redial and put her ear to the letter box. It was ringing, sounded like it was coming from upstairs.

"Stu, I know you're in there. We need to talk." She

banged on the door with her fist, getting frustrated. He was clearly in the house, possibly asleep but probably trying to ignore her in the hope she would just go away. Well, she wasn't having it. She wasn't letting him get away with it this time. She walked around the back of the house.

The rear of the property was in a similar state to the front. It needed some love. She banged on the door and stepped back to look upstairs to see if the curtains twitched. There was a pane of glass missing in the kitchen window. She cupped her hands around her face and looked inside. There were two bags on the worktop. One with cans of beer inside and another with what looked like untouched takeaway.

Her heartbeat bumped up a notch. Stu was a slob but a missing pane of glass? No, he hadn't slipped that far. Not yet.

"Stu! Come down and open up."

Jane banged on the back door again and tried the handle. The door opened slowly. Unopened beer, unopened takeaway, a missing window and now an unlocked door. This wasn't right.

She stepped inside. There was liquid on the floor and an opened can. The room smelled of stale beer.

"The back door was open so I've come in. I'm getting worried now, Stu!" She was already thinking about what she would say to him if he challenged her about being inside. The justification was easy, her cop-sense had kicked in as soon as she saw the state of the kitchen.

There were a number of things that could be happening here. Stu could be genuinely ill. He was overweight, an alcoholic, and on some level he was probably dealing with the stress that came with the job. He was prime heart attack material. Or, and this was the one that really made her nervous, there had been a burglary, a burglary gone wrong. At least for Stu.

She racked her baton, stepping out of the kitchen into the lounge. Her sense of unease grew when she saw how neat and tidy the room was. He definitely wouldn't have left a window broken like that.

"Police!" she called out. Her heartbeat was loud in her ears but her voice remained strong. She should call for backup, but how would it look if the whole division turned up with lights flashing and sirens blaring, only to find him drunk and asleep? That would be the end of whatever respect he had left, not to mention his pension.

She walked to the foot of the stairs and paused. The window had gone, that was the entry point, and the back door was unlocked. If it was a break-in then it was a possibility they were already gone. So where did that leave Stu?

She bounded up the stairs and looked to her left. The bathroom was empty and the other bedroom door was wide open, no sign of disturbance in there. She turned to her right and gasped. A sudden and fierce headache ripped through her skull and the world seemed to tilt on its axis.

The door, Stu's bedroom door, was closed but someone had painted something on the white paint.

It was a word which made her stomach lurch and her mouth go dry.

'Boo!'

In red. In blood. In Stu's blood. The exclamation mark stretched to the bottom of the door as the blood dribbled toward the carpet.

She reached down and pushed the red button on her radio. "Any available units to 24 Hillsway." She paused for a second. "And I'll need an ambulance too." There was silence for a few seconds and it seemed absolute, as if the world was taking a breath. Then the emergency call ended and the radio went mad. She was aware of the chatter in the background but it was somewhere else. In another place, not with her and not at that moment.

The baton was cocked on her shoulder and she used it the push the handle down on the door. It moved down easily, the door swinging inward a few inches. It wasn't enough to see fully into the room.

"Stu?" She was holding onto the last bit of hope.

She pushed the door with the baton again. The carpet was too thick and it tried to hold the door in place, but she used both hands and gave it a shove. The door swung in and this time her legs buckled.

Stu was tied to a chair in the corner. He faced a mirror on the wardrobe door which reflected his mutilated face.

Jane ran forward, aware that the carpet beneath her feet was sticky. It was blood, she knew that without looking down, but it didn't matter, she just had to get to him. She had to check his pulse… she needed to make sure he was…

She felt a tear trickle down her cheek and bit down on her lip to stop others coming. There would be time for that later.

She put her fingers on his neck, feeling for the familiar strong rhythm. She kept her eyes on her fingers, she couldn't look at him, she couldn't stand to see him like that. And it was Stu, in that brief moment when she saw his reflection, saw his eyes. They were unmistakable.

"Come on, Stu," she whispered but there was no pulse. How could there be when his throat was open from ear to ear and his blood was soaking into the carpet?

She closed her eyes. The skin under her fingers was cold. Stu had been dead for a while, quite a while.

In the distance she could hear sirens coming. Coming to her, to help her and to help Stu. She reached down and unclipped the radio.

"Units coming to Hillsway, please wait outside for further instructions." She needed the DI and the DCI to come before uniform walked all over the scene. She clipped the radio back into her harness and dialled the DI's number.

There were so many similarities to the scene at Newman's house. Not least of all the bright orange wig and the blue and white striped costume that Stu was wearing. It was hideous.

6

An airplane engine scraping through the sky was the only sound from the outside world. I could do with a holiday, thought Ben. Somewhere warm, where the weather never really got cold enough to wear a sweater. That would do him nicely. It might stop him getting colds. It might stop him getting tonsillitis.

He rolled over and took the glass of water from the bedside table. He looked at it like it was the enemy which in a way it was, at least to his throat. Anything going down there was treated like a hostile invasion force and had the potential to be expelled by any means possible.

He wasn't supposed to take any painkillers for another two hours, but he popped two out of the blister pack and swallowed them anyway. He gagged but they stayed down. At least for now.

Was it getting any better? It didn't feel like it. The fever was burning too hot, making him do things he couldn't remember doing and leaving dirty great black spots in his memory.

One thing he did remember was calling his local surgery, only to be told "The doctor hasn't got any appointments this week, but we can fit you in late next week. Shall I put you in for the twenty-sixth at four-thirty?"

"It's really bad." He'd forced a cough out in the hope she could hear how bad it was.

"Well, I *could* squeeze you in at four o'clock on the twenty-sixth. Is that any good?"

He'd told her it wasn't any good and that it was a disgrace and that the NHS should be ashamed. He'd started to tell her that he was coming to the surgery whether they had an appointment for him or not, but she hung up before he could finish.

Finding the half-written manuscript on his keyboard had been the last straw. After the initial shock of seeing the pages all neatly piled on the keyboard, his toes had stung and it was then he realised he'd dropped his drink. He stared at the papers for quite some time before building the courage to pick them up. He didn't even remember coming into the office, let alone typing out several thousand words and printing them off. He had been ill, he still was, but losing his memory like that was strange to say the least.

He had nearly dropped them all when he read the first line.

'Sparkles was not dead. In fact, Sparkles felt more alive than he had ever been before. Boo!'

He read the first two pages and then took the rest up to bed with a fresh drink. The spelling and grammar were atrocious, but his first drafts were always usually pretty bad and he was clearly delirious when he wrote it. The style was all his though, there was no disputing that.

Sparkles, though? Why did he decide to reprise that character when the idea so repulsed him last night? He had wanted to dismantle the door chime and more or less burn everything he possessed involving clowns. Hadn't he wanted to pull the book from the publishers too?

But... it was good. The premise of the story was excellent. Didn't Joanne say the book was flying off the shelves? Maybe now was the time to strike and put some money back in the old coffers. The clown appearing in his dream like that wasn't a random mirage generated by the policeman's visit and his own thoughts. It had been created by his subconscious, telling him this was what he should write.

Only once before had he written while drunk, and the results were appalling. When he read it back two days later, after the hangover cleared, he could see it was an incomprehensible stream of consciousness and had filed it in the bin immediately. This was different. Although he couldn't remember typing a single letter, just like when he had been drunk, the story was good.

Sparkles The Clown was alive. His rebirth was as gruesome and vivid as his death. And okay, so it was inspired by the real-life murder on the news, but hadn't Sparkles been born from Gacy in the first place anyway? The policeman's ugly visit, the delirious hallucination in the night and the book doing so well all came together to provoke the part of his brain which had been dormant for so long into action again.

He might have to be careful with the timing of the release. It could be considered bad taste if he got it wrong. Joanne and the publishers would have to talk about that later. At that exact moment, all he could think about was getting the story down.

Ben rolled onto his back. That was two days ago and he hadn't been able to write anything since. Not in fevered delirium or otherwise. It was the same old story. Start something and then run out of steam after the first couple of chapters. Would he ever be able to write anything again, decent or otherwise? It wasn't looking too promising.

The manuscript was on the bed next to him. Some of the sheets were crumpled now. He must have rolled onto them in the middle of the night. Sharing a bed with a clown was no less problematic than sharing it with a woman.

He pushed them together and slowly edged himself out of bed. Other than some toast, he hadn't been able to stomach anything else to eat and his legs were shaky. He'd given serious thought to pissing in the bed to avoid having to get out, but things were bad enough without stinking too. Besides, he could hear Stan whimpering downstairs, and cleaning up his mess was definitely not an option.

"I'll be there in a minute." He tried to shout but his voice sounded more frog and less human. Nevertheless, the dog stopped moaning.

He padded across the floor and walked into the bathroom. All over his body, nerve endings were screaming abuse at him for forcing them into action. He grimaced and stood in front of the mirror, then grimaced again at his appearance. It was shocking how bad he looked, how dark the rings under his eyes were and how pale his skin was. His nose stood out as the only spot of brightness on his face. It was bright red and angry. He almost looked like a clown. A very ill clown.

He had to lean against the wall to steady himself as he used the toilet, but when his mobile rang he jumped, covering his leg in urine. He ignored it while he dabbed the wet patch with toilet paper. Then it rang again and he knew who it was. True to form, Joanne would just keep ringing until he answered it.

It wasn't until her fourth call that he reached the phone. He accepted it and lay back on the bed. It felt cold and damp.

"Number one, numero uno, my friend!"

"Really? That's… that's… well it's good." He couldn't even drum up enthusiasm for news like that. Even though it had been at least five years since his last number one.

"You could at least try to sound happy."

"I am, I just feel like shit."

"Man-flu eh? Well you better get better soon, they want a sequel, they want Sparkles back."

"The publishers? You don't think it's distasteful, do you?" A little surge of excitement fizzed through his ruined body. The first chapter was good but with the well being dry for the last couple of days, he didn't want to commit. He couldn't.

"Distasteful? Not at all. We just need to make sure the timing's right. When can you start?"

Joanne had been patient with him this year, the publishers too. He told her he was writing a sequel to Howl, but that was well over six months ago and she stopped asking about it two months ago. He wanted to give her something. He was by far her biggest client and if he went down then she would too.

"Well, I've started something. I think it's pretty good. I've got some ideas about where it's going and it should work." The first two sentences were true, as far as he could remember anyway, but the second was just a lie. He regretted it straight away.

"You have?" She sounded cautious. "That's brilliant. You just need to stay on track with this one. Not like…"

"Like Howl, you mean?"

"Yes, like Howl." She replied immediately and it stung him even though it was well deserved.

"I'm trying, Jo." He had been, too. For the last two years.

"I know. When you feel better I'll bring you some bubbly to celebrate. Well done, you!"

She hung up but Ben held the phone to his ear for a while afterwards. After that burst of energy, he felt too tired to move.

Stan whined and whistled. The only time he ever barked was when Ben picked him up from the kennel, and even then he looked apologetic afterwards, as if the emotion had got the better of him. Whining *and* whistling was pretty high up on the list of urgent requests. Stan couldn't be ignored any longer.

He let the dog out of the back door and watched him slope

off. Sometimes he looked more like a horse than a dog. He stared at him for few minutes in a daze, and then went to the office to switch on the computer. In the good old days, he couldn't wait to start writing every morning. Some nights he would lie in bed running through plotlines and scenes in his head, filled with so much excitement that it would take hours for him to get to sleep. He would sit down with his paper and pen, and later a computer, and already have a thousand words ready to go in his head. They were exciting and productive times.

Before this bout of flu he still couldn't sleep, but it was for different reasons. For most of the last two years he spent countless nights searching for new stories, trying to force them through the foggy, mysterious magic of his brain. When they failed to come, he started worrying about how he was going to pay the bills. How would he avoid hitting the bottle like his dad? And, as stupid as it sounded, how he would be able to buy Stan his breakfast?

Clownz might be doing well now and that would help matters, but it wasn't a long-term solution to his problems. A film deal would make all of those worries go away completely, but he wasn't willing to let them butcher the story and turn Howl into something it wasn't; something fashionable and ultimately weak.

The real solution was to start writing again. To get something, anything, finished. That was the answer. To be a writer again.

He powered up the PC and opened the word processor. His stomach was in knots and the pain in his throat seemed to grow in intensity.

"Chapter Three." He always whispered as he wrote or typed. He spoke the words louder this time, as if being more vocal would give him the momentum to continue.

His fingers hovered over the keyboard. He bit his lip.

"Sparkles," he announced as he typed the letters, and then stopped. What was next? What did this Newman guy do after he cut the clown's face off? He was a damaged man, a badly damaged and disturbed man who seemed capable of almost anything, just like the original Sparkles. But what was his motivation?

He almost pressed another letter but stopped, clasped his hands together over his stomach. At least this illness had thrown a few of the extra pounds he was carrying. He blew a raspberry at the screen and gave it the finger.

Words, words, words. They were such simple things, but in the mind of a writer they were as precious as the rarest of jewels. Writing a story was like crafting a beautiful necklace made from diamonds, rubies and emeralds, then linking them together with the finest, most delicate golden thread.

All he seemed capable of at the moment, at least when he was conscious, was making one link of a rusty bicycle chain.

He got up, closed it down and shuffled into the kitchen. He could see Stan's tail wagging through the frosted glass of the back door so he let him in. The dog charged straight past to his bowl and started eating. Oh, to be a dog, thought Ben and watched Stan attack his food.

Ben's eyes were drawn to the bottles of spirits on the worktop. He knew from memory what was there. Whisky, gin, vodka and a half-bottle of Navy rum. He never touched them, not after seeing his dad drink his way through the last ten years of his wretched life. Rachel had bought them for guests but there were no guests any longer. They kept away when she left. Not that he missed them, they were all dickheads, but he missed her and he missed writing.

As he stared at the bottle of whisky, the pale sunlight trickled through the window and landed on the amber liquid. A little magic star winked off the bottle and twinkled in his eyes.

The star seemed to whisper to him, 'There's magic this way, come and play. Come here and see.'

He took a mug out of the cupboard and poured a decent measure of whisky into it. Wasn't scotch supposed to be medicinal anyway? He took a sip and grimaced. It scorched a new ravine into his throat and attacked everything in its path as it slipped down his throat. The pain forced him to close his eyes but as the burning sensation turned into a pleasurable warmth in his belly, he sighed and opened his eyes again.

He looked down at the dog who was looking up at him. "This is good stuff, Stanley, me old pal."

He tipped the bottle and filled the mug up to halfway. "What say we go upstairs, put a crappy film on and maybe we can have a nap?"

The dog walked toward the stairs in agreement and Ben followed behind. He hoped the bottle wasn't lying when it said there was magic to be had. He could do with some magic in his life right now.

He lay on the bed and patted Rachel's side for Stan to

climb up. The dog wouldn't get on the bed unless the invitation was made clear and even then he seemed to consider the request as if it might be a trap of some sort.

"Come on, I thought we were watching a film?" He patted the duvet again and the dog stared at the bed, waiting for a surprise ambush. He looked up at Ben again and clambered up.

He was a tall dog but skinny and as a result very bony. He turned around a few times, curled up and grumbled.

Ben stroked his head slowly. "There you go, big fella, that's got to be better than the floor."

Stan licked his dog-lips and closed his eyes.

"Now, what's on at half-past ten on a Wednesday morning?" Ben took the remote control and pointed it at the television. It was clearly not prime time and there were mostly programmes about houses; selling, building and renovating them. He sipped the whisky and surfed the channels.

He had underestimated what drinking whisky on an empty stomach before noon did to a person. His eyes took a moment to focus each time he flicked to the next channel. Rachel hated it when he channel-surfed, but then again she hated almost everything about him by the end. Not that he blamed her, he pretty much hated himself too.

He pushed through the stations, seeing only a blurry image of what was on until he flicked past a picture of a clown. He flicked back immediately.

It was the news channel and they were showing a poor-quality YouTube video. It was little more than a slide show of Harvey Newman as Bingo The Clown in a variety of poses with children at parties. Some of them were obviously digitally reproduced Polaroids from years ago while some looked to be more recent. Most of the kids looked happy but some looked at Sparkles with horror. Or maybe Ben was just seeing things, now he knew what the clown was actually like.

The reporter urged families to come forward to speak to police, particularly if they recognised any of the videos on Newman's YouTube channel.

Ben could feel his eyes growing heavier by the minute, but he took another sip and felt the lessening bite of the drink slide down his throat. It momentarily woke him up again but it was a losing battle, he knew it.

He closed his eyes. In the background, he could hear a reporter talking about another murder. A police officer this time but details were just coming in…

Stan chattered his teeth, thumped his tail on the bed and kicked his back legs as he ran around the track in his dreams. Maybe he won the race this time.

Ben smiled and put his hand on the dog's neck. It was woolly and comforting. A moment later, he fell asleep.

*

Sore throat? Check. Stiff neck? Check. Throbbing head? Check. Chattering teeth and a low-pitched whine? Check. It could only mean he was awake again. Awake with another hangover and Stan needed to go out. How long had he been asleep? There was no way of knowing unless he opened his eyes and he wasn't ready to do that yet.

Ben touched his brow with his fingertips and felt a horrible cold, sticky sweat. The whisky had been okay at the time but now it was only amplifying the pain in his body. Was he really awake or was this just a terrible nightmare?

He felt his mind closing down again; cog by cog, it was shutting down. That was good, he needed to sleep.

Stan whined again but it was louder this time. Ben moved his hand across the bed to find him.

"Go back to sleep, boy," he whispered.

Stan whimpered at the sound of his voice, but the dog wasn't on the bed and he wasn't at the foot of the bed either. He was next to Ben's head.

He rolled onto his side and reached out. "Too early, Stan, too early, kiddo." He touched the dog's head and immediately opened his eyes. The dog wasn't just trembling, as he did when he was cold, he was vibrating. Their eyes met for a moment and Ben saw a slice of moonlight reflected off his beautiful, clear pupils. Stan looked away and whined again. It was a high-pitched sound that hurt Ben's ears.

"Come on, back to sleep." He felt sleepy and disorientated. Dealing with a neurotic dog was the last thing he needed.

Stan turned his head back to Ben but as their eyes met again, the dog snapped his head around and looked away. He looked toward the opposite side of the room, toward the window. The dog curled his lip and growled.

Ben went cold all over.

He was aware of his own breathing. It was laboured and wheezy, and there was now a tightness in his chest that hadn't been there yesterday. Today? Last night? When was it? Without any routine, time had become unimportant.

But as well as his own breathing, there was the sound of another's breath in the room. And not that of the dog trembling beside the bed.

The effort of rolling over was nearly too much for his aching and weak body, but he managed it. He rolled slowly but as he did, the room became a dizzying blur, as if he were on a carousel spinning at a hundred miles an hour. It was a sickening sensation and his stomach turned a somersault, threatening to expel what little food was in there.

The bathroom flew past and then the enormous built-in wardrobes skidded across his vision. He felt as if he was no longer in control of his eyes as they fought to bring focus to what he was seeing.

A shape emerged on the far side of the room, in the corner where the wardrobes ended. Ben felt all of the moisture in his mouth vanish. It was sucked back into his body, retreating away from something.

His mind searched for a rational explanation but it too was struggling to stay focused.

It was the shape of a human, a man. He was standing in the corner of the room, looking into the corner, like a naughty child in the classroom. Stan growled again.

The moon shone in through the window and illuminated only half of the intruder's head. It was a dream or a hallucination conjured up by his fevered brain. Nothing more.

"Go away," Ben croaked.

But he wasn't staring into the corner, was he? No, he was staring into the built-in mirror on the wardrobe. The floor-to-ceiling design Rachel had requested. He was staring at his own reflection.

Ben squinted, trying to bring it into focus. It was a face. An ugly, pale face with black painted diamonds running vertically over eye sockets. It was make-up, it was clown's make-up and it was bleeding down its face.

The clown bared his teeth in an attempt at a smile. It was the most frightening thing Ben had ever seen. Even in the gloom, he could see the clown's teeth were discoloured and the skin around his mouth didn't stretch, it cracked, releasing a thin watery fluid.

The clown breathed hard onto the mirror and his blue hands wrote *BOO!* in the fog.

Ben groaned as the clown turned around and walked slowly out of the room. Not once did he turn to look at Ben again, he just strolled out of the room like he was on a Sunday afternoon amble. He watched the clown go with eyes that felt like they were constantly rolling over and over and over in their sockets.

He wanted to vomit. He wanted to throw his guts up but he knew if he tried to walk across the bedroom, he wouldn't get more than two steps. His legs were gone, they were jelly. The clown's footsteps retreated down the stairs and he heard the front door open and then close. Not with a sudden bang like someone running but slowly, casually.

Stan whined and his teeth bounced together, not in a gentle or soothing way but with a loud smashing that was born from fear. Ben reached out to touch him but the dog was already clambering up onto the bed on top of him. The dog lay down with a grunt and put his head on Ben's chest.

He could feel Stan shaking. It was uncomfortable on his body but he stroked the dog's head. It was as much to comfort himself.

"A ghost," he said as his mind offered something usable. He'd written about them often enough. Hell, he'd written three books trying to scare readers witless with them. It was just a ghost, that was all. These old farmhouse conversions must be full of them.

"Just a ghost, Stan. They can't hurt us. Not really." His voice broke in several places and came out as a breath, like a sigh. He had been thinking about clowns too much. With writing a sequel, it had been on his mind.

He looked at the mirror. Where the word *BOO!* had been written just seconds before was now just a dark mirror. The word had disappeared because it was never there. 'Boo!' was what Sparkles always said to his victims just before he killed them. Just before he ate their brains and stole their smiles for himself.

And the ghost *had* looked a little bit like Sparkles, hadn't he? A Sparkles who was very ill. Sicker even than he was.

He left his hand on Stan's head and closed his eyes. They still felt like they were barrelling around in his head but at least there were no ghosts to see now. No more clowns smiling back from the mirror at him.

7

The doctor had put Ben on citalopram for depression. That was about a month ago and it was the reason he'd been able to do the book signing. Nobody knew about it of course, but who was there to tell anyway?

He wasn't a 'New Man', nor had he ever really been in touch with his 'feminine side' or any of those other clichéd or outdated terms. He didn't cry, men didn't cry, at least not until last year, then men cried a lot. Ben Night, specifically, had cried every single day for nearly a whole year.

The first time he cried, he felt strangely liberated by the experience. At the age of forty-seven there weren't many new experiences, at least legal and physical ones, but crying was just that. Crying was something new, and it felt exciting and slightly dangerous.

He was watching The Fellowship of the Ring in bed while eating a bag of cheesy Doritos and drinking beer. The scene where Boromir died clutching his sword brought about a great tide of grief and a flood of tears. It was completely unexpected and extremely shocking. He had watched the film scores of times before, but never once had it elicited such an emotional response.

Stan had shuffled nervously on the bed as Ben laughed with tears streaming down his face. He was liberated and he thought for a while that he might be a 'New Man' or in touch with his 'feminine side'. He even telephoned Rachel to tell her, but she had changed her number and the recorded message told him the line was no longer active.

The novelty wore off after two weeks, even with Stan who was usually a very patient dog. He would leave the room when the crying started, whether that be in the middle of the day or the middle of the night. It had no respect for location either.

He'd cried in the bank, behind the wheel of the car, in bed, and once when he was taking a crap. When the tears came, they came hard and there was usually little or no reason for them. They just needed to be out of his system.

It didn't take long for him to realise that the tears were nothing to do with finding himself; they were a sign of something more serious, something damaging. But Mr Ego was shouting loud, above the voice of Mr Reason, and he talked Ben out of a visit to the doctors. Mr Ego told him to pull his socks up and get on with it, get on with writing that next story before someone else stole it away. But the more he sat at the computer, staring with blurry eyes through lack of sleep, the worse things got. Fewer words appeared on the screen each day and the river of unending ideas – which had always run through his head, house, garden and the world beyond – dried up. It became barren. It became dead, just like him.

He'd thought about suicide. Several times. It seemed every time his eyes focused on the knife-block, he thought about it. What would it be like to take one of those polished steel handles and draw the blade across his throat? How would it feel to bleed himself dry? But at those times, Stan seemed to watch him. Standing beneath the knife-block with his big, brown, sad eyes staring up at him as if to say, *'Don't you dare, I haven't had my breakfast!'* And then more tears would come and he'd end up sitting on the kitchen floor with a hungry greyhound nuzzling his hand. If it wasn't for the dog, he might have done more than just consider it.

When Joanne rang and told him he was pencilled in to do a book signing, there was just enough of him left to reach down the phone and grasp her voice. Just enough to hear her read a fan letter from someone who said Ben's books had changed his life, reformed and given him a new purpose. It was from an ex-con, an ex-addict. On some level that appealed to him.

That was when Ben made an appointment to see the doctor. That was when he spent half an hour snivelling, crying and wailing and everything came out. His guilt over his affairs and his terrible treatment of Rachel, the loss of his self-respect over that, the loss of motivation, the lack of joy, and the total and utter demise of his creativity.

After the visit, he definitely did feel like the fabled 'New Man'. When the medication kicked in, it lifted him off the kitchen floor and dropped him back in the office. There had been ideas, there had even been a chapter or two, but that was as far as it went. He hadn't cried since that day. Except once when he again watched Boromir say, "I would have followed you, my brother. My captain. My king." It was an emotional scene, after all. The medication relieved the depression, but it couldn't work magic and fan the creative spark that had all but gone out.

But now Ben cried. He stood by his computer and the tears fell silently down his cheeks. These were tears of relief, utter relief and joy. There were words again, a sheaf of papers all covered in beautiful words sitting neatly on the keyboard. Exactly where they had been last time.

He picked them up and started reading. Maybe drinking whisky wasn't such a bad idea after all.

*

After reading for an hour, Ben slid the papers onto his desk and looked out of the little window. It faced onto a patchwork of fields which stretched up toward the horizon. There was only one other house in sight, so far away it looked as big as a Lego block.

This writing wasn't his. Nor was the first part of the story. Neither were on his hard drive or backed up on his memory stick, and even in a confused delirium he would have saved his words. It only took one lost or accidentally deleted book to instil that into a writer.

So that left one person who could be responsible. The ghost, the fevered spirit his mind had conjured up.

The clown. The clown had been in his house, not once but twice.

The shudder that thought sent through his body made him groan involuntarily, and he stood up. He needed to call the police and report it. He walked through the kitchen toward the front room, pausing in the hall to lock the front door. In all the years he lived there, he had never worried about closing let alone locking the doors. He picked up the phone and hovered over the digits. What exactly was he going to say to them?

"Hello, I'd like to report a burglary."

"When did it happen?"

"Last night. In the middle of the night. I don't know when exactly because I've been ill and I drank too much whisky to help me sleep."

"Okay, so what was stolen?"

"Well, nothing."

"Right, so what happened?"

"A clown broke in with some stories he's written, and he dropped them off for me. He wrote 'Boo!' on my wardrobe mirror, but that's gone now so you can't see it."

"Maybe you ought to lay off the whisky, Mr Night?"

He fell onto the sofa head-first and buried his face in the cushion. He stayed that way for a minute until the thought of the fat copper's arse pressing into the fabric moved him. What the hell was going on here? Had he finally lost his marbles?

No, he had flu, tonsillitis and probably a chest infection, but his marbles were all still there rattling around in his head. This was just weird.

He grabbed the remote and put the television on. It was

as much to see what time it was as anything else. The light coming into the room from the front window seemed to be the same at all times of the day. Grey.

The box came to life on the news channel where he'd left it after the copper visited. He'd been an obnoxious idiot and didn't look capable of catching anyone, let alone a murderer. Ben flicked off the channel as they were going live to a scene outside someone's house. It was just babble to him, so he tapped in the number for sports news and watched it with an equal measure of gloom for a few seconds.

He switched it off again and listened to the wind squeezing into some unknown gap in the eaves. Rachel hated the sound, she said it was the noise ghosts made. He'd lost count of the number of tradesmen she asked to locate and repair whatever it was, but none of them could, of course. Old buildings, even renovated ones, liked to have a secret or two.

The sound didn't bother him. In fact he quite liked it, especially when the wind brought the rain across the fields and dashed it against the windows. That was fine by him and it suited his writing somehow. Used to, anyway.

The writing in his office was good. It wouldn't win any prizes for literature but the ideas for a story were there. If he could make it more cohesive, it had the beginnings of a decent book. There needed to be more of course, lots more but it was there and more importantly, the cogs had started turning again. Slowly and with plenty of creaking and groaning but they were moving. With a bit of lubrication he could make them shine.

Ben could feel the first signs of excitement in his stomach. That's where it always started but it had been a while. That little tickle and flutter that titillated his body with the promise there would be bigger, better and altogether more satisfying sensations just around the corner. It was a drug. A drug which he was addicted to. It was one which he had been going cold turkey on for the last couple of years.

He got up from the sofa, wobbling as his head swam and his vision narrowed. He was dehydrated and hungry but he didn't want to eat or drink, he just wanted to get to the book and start drafting out the first few chapters.

He walked slowly out of the lounge, but paused by the front door and put his hand on the key. If the intruder, whoever he was, wanted to hurt Ben, he'd been given ample opportunity to do just that. He had been in a stupor for a good portion of the last week and asleep for most of the last twenty-four hours. It was creepy, but he wasn't here to hurt Ben, seemingly he was here to help him.

Ben turned it over in his mind. It was a fan, that was all. A fan who wanted to see his favourite character reprised in a new story. A collaboration? A joint effort with an unknown writer who just happened to look like an ugly clown? A collaboration with Sparkles? He shivered. What a hideous thought. The writer had some skill but what he'd written wasn't good enough to publish. It certainly wasn't good enough to allow him access to the house.

He shivered again, walked to his office, picked up the bundle of papers and a pen. If he did a second draft of what was already written and put some Ben Night flourishes into the words, then it would grease the wheels a little more.

He walked back upstairs, re-reading the opening paragraphs.

"Sparkles finished tying the policeman to the chair and stood behind him. He put him in front of the mirror so he could see both of their reflections as he worked. Observing the victim's face as he killed him was easy but observing his own was trickier. He wanted to see his own smile widen as the blood of the policeman spurted from his body.

"He tilted his head and looked at his face. He didn't look good, he was looking ill, particularly where his nose was now deflated and… well, pale. The policeman's nose was red, it was bright red and bulbous.

"He pushed the tip of the blade into one of his nostrils and felt the officer flinch. 'Boo!' he whispered into his ear. He could already feel his smile growing as he started cutting…"

When Ben read the words 'policeman' and 'officer', his mind showed him a picture of DC Kelly sitting in the chair, looking into his own reflection as the clown cut him to bits. He fell onto the bed and smiled. He had killed police officers, both male and female, in his other stories but never people he'd actually met. Never people he actually disliked. This made it more powerful. More real.

He read through the first page, making changes here and there, removing extra words that were unnecessary. The cogs were lubricated, not with oil but with blood. Just how he liked it.

If he was going to write another story about Sparkles, clowns and the circus, he might need to contact Jim Crawley for the purposes of research. Not that he liked the man, he was cringeworthy, but what he didn't know about clowns and the circus wasn't worth knowing.

8

Maldon liked colouring in. As far as he could remember, he had always liked it. One of his earliest memories was sitting on the carpet in the lounge, colouring in a picture of a fire engine. He had coloured it in red felt-tip pen, the brightest red in his pencil case, and it had been so dazzling that he thought the whole page might be burning in front of his eyes.

Even in the darkest moments of his life, before he found Ben Night's books at least, he had coloured in. It didn't have to be pictures, although he always preferred that. In the days of heroin, colouring books had been low on the list of priorities so he coloured on his skin. He covered his arms in wavy, vivid designs in the brightest colours he could imagine. He coloured other people's flesh too. Sometimes when they were asleep, sometimes when they were awake and sometimes when they were in that in-between state that heroin gave them.

Nobody minded. Nobody ever minded because the

colours were so bright and cheerful. It was light when their whole world was a grey, stinking swamp.

"There!" He put down the felt-tip pen and picked up the mask to admire his work. "That's much better."

"Well, if I could see it I could give you an honest opinion. I warn you, I'm not going out looking like a fool!"

"I wouldn't do that!" He was slightly hurt by the suggestion.

"Let me see then. This very instant!"

Maldon sighed and put the Sparkles mask back on. He was extremely pleased with his efforts and he knew Sparkles would be too. He walked to the bathroom and stood in front of the mirror.

"There. Happy?" he asked.

"Oh, I say!" Sparkles announced. *"Turn to the side."*

Maldon did as he was instructed.

"Oh yes, now turn the other way. Quite delightful. Honk, honk!" Sparkles laughed like Muttley on the biggest dose of amphetamines anyone had ever consumed.

The fat policeman's nose had been bulbous. But it hadn't been red enough for Sparkles and so Maldon had been instructed to colour it bright crimson. It was a task he didn't mind, and spent the last hour taking care not to go out of the lines and spoil everything. He had even touched up the diamond shapes on either side of his eyes.

He had no idea how women put make-up on in the mirror, because after he had cut out the old, saggy nose and glued the policeman's nose on, he put Sparkles on his face and tried to colour it in while looking at his reflection.

Sparkles had been irritating and kept trying to issue further instructions, criticising him when his hands moved in the wrong direction. In the end he had to put Sparkles on the floor and tell him to shut up while he went into his *colouring-in world.*

He took the policeman's smile too. He cut it out and gave it to Sparkles, just like he wanted. It was wider than it had been before he killed the policeman but it wasn't as wide as it should be.

Sparkles had been irritating in the copper's house too. Telling him what to do, when to do it and even shouting at him in front of the policeman. The officer had wet himself when they were arguing like that. He was clearly upset about the whole episode and he had every right to be.

But all had been forgotten when they were in front of the mirror working with the knife. The copper screamed and Sparkles laughed and they had all been bathed in blood. His stinking, piggy blood.

"Is that better? Are you happier?" he asked.

Sparkles's features drooped to one side, like it was sliding off his face.

"Do I look it?"

"Not really but I'm trying." Sparkles was only secured by two rubber bands which were threaded through the mask and then hooked over his ears. It was uncomfortable and the mask slipped from side to side as he walked. It didn't look good.

"I'd like for us to be closer. That would make me happier. Not entirely happy mind you, but happier."

Maldon felt his spirits lift. Sparkles was demanding but he genuinely wanted for them to be as close as possible.

"Why don't you take that little tube of superglue under there and hitch us together like an old married couple?"

He looked at the tube of glue on the floor under the sink. Someone had once told him that rubbing the stuff all over your fingertips made it impossible for you to leave your prints at a scene. What a load of old rubbish that turned out to be.

He bent down and picked it up.

"Till death do us part, dear Mouldy!" Sparkles squeaked in his high-pitched voice.

"Sure about this?"

In the mirror, Sparkles smile grew, just a few millimetres but it grew nonetheless.

"Does that answer your question?"

Maldon slipped Sparkles off and used the mirror to apply glue to his skin. It stung a little but it would be worth it to see that smile again. He used most of the tube in small dots all over his face, forehead and neck, and when he finished he closed his eyes and pushed Sparkles back on. The music started immediately and it was beautiful, never mind that the key was all wrong and some of the notes were in the wrong order. It was chaotic, circus music. It was clown music.

He smoothed it out. keeping pressure on his hands until he could feel a cramp starting to build in his forearms. Then he opened his eyes. He looked better than ever and the smile had definitely grown, just a little but it was there, the start of a tilt at the corners. It was still pale but that would come in time too. By the time he'd finished he wouldn't need to colour it in, it would be bright enough and wide enough for Sparkles to be completely happy again. For both of them to be happy again.

9

Things were getting messy for Jane Brady. Firstly, there was her team on Operation Mint – Harvey Newman's murder. Then a second team on the child abuse enquiry, which was growing by the minute. And another team on Stu's murder.

Even though major investigations like this were regionalised, Harvey Newman was taking more than his fair share of resources for both his life and death. Poor old Stu was stretching resources to their limit.

Add to that the number of detectives now working out of one office and things were starting to get confusing, as well as loud. She looked across the room. Someone was already sitting at Stu's desk. Someone she didn't know or recognise.

Jane had been offered counselling, and the DI even offered a few days off. She accepted one but not the other. If she took the counselling, they wouldn't *make* her take the days off. She didn't want or need to be away from the office. What she needed was to get her hands on the sick bastard who had cut Stu's face off; sat him in front of a mirror like he was in a barber's chair and cut him to bits while he watched. They were waiting for the reports, but she hoped to god Stu was long dead before he was carved up.

There were volunteers from all over the force, all over the country, to come and help with the investigation. The officers were willing to work around the clock to catch the killer. She was one of them and would have gladly worked a double shift to help, but they wouldn't allow her to walk away from Bingo the paedophile.

"Jane, you got a minute?" DI White stuck his head around his office door and beckoned her over.

She walked in and sat down. He was usually immaculately dressed, but his shirt was open at the collar and his tie was in a ball on the desk. His chin had a day's worth of growth on it.

"Boss?" she asked.

He looked distracted despite having just called her. He moved his mouse around frantically.

"Yes… sorry, Jane, I'll be right with you."

That irritated her. She had a lot to do and didn't really have the time to sit here waiting for him to finish what he was doing. Why had he called her if he wasn't ready?

"Shall I come back?" she asked, pushing her chair away from the desk.

White flung the mouse to the side. He looked in a bad mood, like she was the one who had disturbed him.

"No, no. Sorry. I'm trying to do too may things at once."

Tell me about it, thought Jane, but she just smiled and nodded.

"I'm going through HOLMES and I can't see what tasks Stu was working on. Have you got them? Chambers wants to see."

DI White had come from Social Services about ten years ago. He'd been a safeguarding manager over there and just decided he fancied a change. He'd gone up two ranks in half the time Jane had gone up one. That fact didn't mean he was a good copper though. He wasn't, he was just good at taking exams and saying the right things to the right people. He was a good, honest man but he was in the wrong job.

She walked around the desk to show him where to find the information. "I've got paper copies of the task sheets if he wants them too, but they're all here." She moved the mouse around the screen quickly to show him exactly where the information was stored.

Nobody had been there to show her how to use HOLMES, she had just learned.

The Home Office Large Major Enquiry System was a computer program through which passed every single piece of information, evidence, exhibit and statement on an enquiry like this. It was designed to eliminate the risk of missing something; some small sliver of evidence upon which the entire investigation could hinge. It was a product of historical mistakes, missed opportunities and miscarriages of justice.

She sat back down on the other side of the desk. "He'd got twelve outstanding enquiries and was just about to go back through the CCTV again." She knew what all of her officers had on their task lists, but had gone over Stu's countless times in the last two days to see if anything would help. Anything that would indicate a pattern.

"I've got a list of his completed tasks too if he wants them?"

"No, it's just these at the moment. Thank you." White spoke while moving the mouse again. He looked tired, really tired and stressed.

He stopped, rubbed his neck and leaned back. "You know they took his computer, don't you?"

It was something that hadn't been mentioned but they all knew about it, each and every one of them.

"I do," she answered, "but Stu…" But what? But Stu wasn't a paedophile? All sorts of hypotheses were being put around the office. Theories which were too strong to ignore because of the MO. Stu Kelly was a lot of things but she hoped to god the computer would come back clean.

"I hope they come back clean." White echoed what she had just been thinking, what the entire force was hoping too.

"Will you let me know?" She was Stu's last supervisor so under normal circumstances would be kept in the loop, but this was different. His murder was being handled by a different team and they wouldn't automatically inform her unless it had a bearing on the Bingo case. She knew that whatever was on the computer, whether clean or dirty, would have an impact on her case.

"Of course."

There was silence for a moment and Jane stood up. She thought it was her cue to leave but White started talking.

"Worst case scenario and Stu's computer comes back

dirty, then we'll all be working together anyway. One enormous, happy incident room." His phone rang and he picked it up. "DI White, Incident Room." A pause and then, "On my way."

He put the phone down, sighed and put his tie on. "Thanks for this, Jane. I'll see you in a bit."

She smiled and walked out of his office. He wasn't so bad. At least he left her alone to manage the office, unlike some inspectors she had worked for in the past.

She sat down and looked at her own tasks. She had twice as many as anyone else in the office, but as she looked around she knew how snowed-under they all were. It would be unfair to start dishing out Stu's unfinished enquiries yet, if ever. No, she would take responsibility for them. They were hers now.

She scanned through them and found the CCTV action. It was the most urgent out of the pile, the one Stu had moaned about doing. She remembered their conversation in the briefing room and felt a stab of guilt. He was just seeing out his time, just trying to make it through to the end without getting too dirty along the way. She put her jacket on. She hoped he hadn't covered himself in shit with his computer.

Stu had made copies of all the footage from the night of the clown's murder. She booked it out of the exhibit store and put the first disc into her computer. Stu had found Newman's Ford Focus and traced him from one side of Derby to the other. That wasn't difficult – he had a photograph of his face on the side of his car and his wig billowed like a cloud in the driver's seat. He had driven straight home after a child's party, but Stu lost him before he reached his address. There weren't many cameras in the suburbs and private CCTV had been a washout.

She went back through the footage using the camera-maps Stu had created. For a change, it looked like he'd been thorough. After seven hours, her eyes felt like they were made of spiky fragments of glass. She had checked every angle to see if he'd been followed home, going backwards and forwards trying to pick out number plates on the grainy images. He hadn't been followed, of course he hadn't. Whoever killed him was already there, already waiting for him.

It was a needle in a haystack.

"You going home?"

She jumped and looked up. DI White was standing over her. The office was empty except for the two of them

"Soon, I just want to finish this." The screen said it was close to ten o'clock and the sky outside said it was ten o'clock at night, not the morning.

"His computer's clean," White said.

Jane looked back up and they both smiled. "Brilliant," she said, a wave of relief washing over her.

"Thought you might like to know. I'll see you in the morning, I'm going home for the first time in two days."

"Night, boss."

White walked into his office and came out a minute later holding his jacket. "Don't stay late, Jane."

She held her hand up. "I won't. Night."

"Night." He waved and walked off down the corridor. It was never totally quiet in a police station at any time, but for the first time in days the office felt truly empty.

She ejected a disc and put the last one in. After this she was going home. She was going to take a long hot bath, drink two icy-cold bottles of beer and read her book. Thank god there were no irritating or needy men to spoil it. She'd worked with enough of them to last her a lifetime. That part of the evening would be bliss but the chances of sleeping well were nil. There was too much going round and round in her head for that.

The disc clunked into life. Soon they would be obsolete and everything digital, but the force might actually need to splash out on an upgrade for that to work. The last twenty years had gone by in a flash but she loved every minute of it. Well, perhaps not *every* minute of it. There had been some low points but this was where she wanted to be, where she always wanted to be. It was corny and it was cheesy, but doing this job mattered. It was an important job and as a police officer, people looked to you for help. If you couldn't give them that help, then you had no business pretending to be a copper.

She moved the pointer around the screen, trying to find something, anything, to grab at. This footage was later than the estimated time of death. Stu would have looked at it but without being given a registration or even a car make or model, he was just fishing in the dark.

Stu had been right to be grumpy about it. The task was long, unglamorous and fruitless. They needed something more to work with.

"What's that?" she whispered and leaned in closer.

Her eyes were dry and she rubbed them to stimulate her focus. A car, an old one, pulled up at a set of traffic lights. The interior of the car was too dark and the driver's head just a black blob, but across the road, a man was sticking large posters to the wall. There was no mistaking the image of a clown or the word 'circus' in big red letters across the posters. So the circus was in town, was it? She disliked the circus as much as she disliked clowns. She wouldn't be paying them a visit any time soon.

She looked away from the poster to the car at the lights and gasped. It wasn't that the car was too dark to see inside, it was that the driver had been looking at the posters too. He turned around slowly and looked directly at the camera with a vile and pained grimace on his face. It was hideous, like a horror film, and the blurry footage made him look like a ghost. There were dark shapes around his eyes, like distorted and stretched diamonds running down his pasty face. And then he was gone.

The car pulled away but Jane didn't move. Her body was frozen. She didn't believe what she had just seen. It couldn't be right. Her eyes were tired and somehow the poster clown had become superimposed over the driver's face. That was all.

She let go of her breath, unaware until then that she had been holding it. She needed those beers more than she thought. She moved the slider back, found the image of the poster-boy sticking his posters to the wall then started the footage rolling again.

"Circus posters, dark car." She talked her way through the scene. "Driver obscure, turns his head…"

She watched as his face came into view. Just as he grimaced, his teeth clearly on show as if he were snarling at her, she heard laughter from somewhere and jumped. She was immediately embarrassed. It was someone down the corridor, in the parade room, that was all.

She wound it back again and paused it on the driver's face. She had one of Bingo's promotional flyers on her desk somewhere and she rifled through the paperwork until she found it. She held it next to the screen. The same black diamonds around the eyes.

The driver was wearing Harvey Newman's face. Bingo was alive again.

She touched the screen. "Boo!" she whispered. The motive for killing Newman had appeared clear. A grown-up victim come to get revenge, but apart from Stu being involved in the investigation there didn't seem to be a connection.

She went back through the footage and tried to read the number plate, but part of it was intentionally obscured. Only the last two letters were clear. This needed further work. The intelligence guys would be able to do some searches on partial plates and some geek would know what sort of car it was. It wasn't a new shape, that was for sure.

She printed the clearest image and stared at it. His twisted face was one of the creepiest things she had ever seen.

It wasn't perfect by any means. It was a long way off that but it was a start, something concrete at last. A picture in her hands of the killer and his car, albeit probably a stolen one. She tried to smile but her tired muscles could only form a scowl.

*

Jane was already at her desk by the time White came in. She had been there for nearly two hours and it wasn't quite seven o'clock.

"Have you been home, Jane?" He strolled over, the smell of his aftershave preceding him.

"Have a look at this." She didn't answer his question although she had been home, just not slept much.

He took the still image off her and looked at it. "What is this?"

"It's Bingo, or rather it's his face. Harvey Newman's face."

"Is it?" White asked. He didn't sound convinced.

Jane did her best not to sound exasperated. She handed him Bingo's flyer. "Look that the eyes."

There was a pause before he spoke again. She watched him look from one picture to the other in rapid succession.

"Ah, I see it now. The quality's shit. That's one creepy grin." He handed both items back to her.

"I've got the team looking at the car," she said. "Looks like it's a 1986 Austin Metro in blue. Twelve possibilities with the visible numbers present and none local. One reported stolen from Dorset two months ago." It was concise information that she knew most bosses loved. No waffle, just facts.

"Seems like you've got it under control. Have we spoken with Dorset yet?"

Jane nodded. "Just waiting for a call-back from the shift sergeant to tell me about the car theft."

She could feel adrenalin rampaging through her body. They just needed a bit of luck with the car theft, something to give the whole team a boost.

"Okay, let me know when you get the info and we'll go and see the DCI together. Good work, Jane."

Jane smiled as White walked away. She didn't need praise but it didn't hurt. She looked at the image of Bingo smiling at the camera and winced. He would probably look worse in the flesh than he did on the image. It was a grim thought, a grim thought indeed.

10

Two shows down, three to go. Then they would move on to another dump and the fun and laughter would start all over again. Woohoo!

Jim Crawley opened a can of cider and drained half of it in one go. He winced, it was barely cool. The fridge in his caravan was on the blink again, which was hardly surprising given that it was over twenty years old and held together by tape. He finished the rest of the can and started on another. He couldn't afford a new caravan or fridge. Maybe if he used a touch of gentle persuasion on Denise, she might have a quiet word in Fred's ear about giving him a pay rise.

Screwing the boss's wife was uninspiring in a physical sense but over the years it had given him leverage. When Fred wanted to fire him for letting the generator run dry, Denise had been there to talk him out of it. When Fred wanted to let him go for fighting with one of the clowns, Denise had been kind enough to dissuade him. It seemed Denise valued her marriage and the thought of Crawley sharing their dirty little secret with Fred scared the crap out of her.

It didn't scare him so much, he could take care of Fred anytime he wanted. Ten years ago, things might have been different. Fred was a fighter back then and nasty with it, but he could take him now, no problem. Ten years of manual labour, putting up the big top and hauling equipment around the various sites had given Jim's body a wiry power. He wasn't big but he was lean, strong and twice as nasty as Fred had ever been. A few drunken brawls with other technicians and some memorable fights with townies had only built on the fighting skills he'd learned growing up. No, just let Fred try and take him on, then he'd find out what sort of a nasty bastard he had working for him.

There was a bang on the flimsy door of his caravan. He didn't get up. "What?" he yelled.

"Creep... Jim, the generator's packed up again. Fred wants you to fix it tonight."

"Wanker," he whispered under his breath. He knew the others called him Creepy Crawley but never to his face. This was as close as anyone had come. He ought to get up and beat the shit out of the kid just for starting to call him that name. He knew who it was though, and kicking the boss's nephew in the face wouldn't go down well.

"Five minutes," he shouted back. Make them wait, that was the way to do it. Make them appreciate him a bit more.

He had purposely sabotaged the generator so it wouldn't work without him, so he was the only one who knew how to fix it. There was nothing wrong with it but he made sure everyone knew how temperamental it was, and always swore when he was repairing it to make it look difficult and infuriating. Sometimes he purposely delayed the show by creating an additional problem with the generator. Hearing people getting inpatient inside the tent made him smile. But what really made him happy was hearing Fred apologising and offering them all a free return ticket the next time they were in town. One day he would force Fred to cancel a whole week's performance, that would be the ultimate in smiles. It was all leverage, that's how the world worked.

He would finish his drink then go and pretend to fix the generator. He might even call on that pretty little acrobat who'd just started with them. He had to get in there quick, he didn't want everyone telling her to avoid him, telling them why they called him Creepy Crawley. He had a week, two tops, before she avoided him like the plague. He smiled to himself. She would be right to avoid him too, he was not a nice man, but so what? It was more fun this way.

Not as much fun as being a clown though. That was the reason he'd come to the lousy circus in the first place – to be a clown. But they wouldn't let him, at least not straight away. They stuck him on the maintenance crew with all the other misfits and drop-outs. Christ, it was like being a kid again, working with that lot of creatures. Fighting, proving yourself and not backing down when the big guy tries to take liberties with you.

Boom, that was the big guy's name. He thought he was a real hard-nut, a tough guy who could use his size to make you back down. Problem was, Jim had met plenty of boys like Boom before and not once had he backed down then, so he sure as hell wasn't going to back down when Boom tried to take his cigarettes off him. Boom was big, but he was slow. After Jim had absorbed four or five big haymakers from him on the arms, he saw a glint of panic in Boom's eyes. It was a little sign that said, '*This guy knows how to fight, he's done it before. What do I do?*' Jim had seen that before too and it was enough to know he had already won the fight.

He bit half of Boom's ear off. When he knelt above the beaten man, he squeezed his cheeks so Boom's mouth opened like a gasping fish, spat the chewy cartilage into his mouth and laughed. It was important to go the extra mile to make people frightened of you. Nobody messed with him after that, but Fred decided he might not have the right temperament to be a clown. Not even when he came up with a great idea for a bad clown, a naughty or nasty one that frightens the kids. Fred hadn't liked that idea much and looked at him like he was a lunatic. That was the moment he decided he would sleep with Denise. Just to spite him; the idea of leverage came later.

There was always room for more clowns, especially the bad ones.

His phone rang and he stared at it for a moment. The screen didn't show a name so he ignored it. It was probably just someone trying to sell him something. At least it wasn't Denise asking him to come over to her caravan while Fred was out. He didn't really want to screw her again, she wasn't his type, she was too easy. He preferred things if they were a little more… difficult.

The call ended and the screen went dark for a minute, then flashed to say there was a message waiting for him. Sales people didn't usually leave messages, especially not at eleven o'clock at night.

He should probably go and fix the generator now. It had been a good ten minutes since the kid knocked on his door. He climbed out of the bed, which he rarely converted back to the two-seater sofa arrangement any longer, and picked up his phone. The van was a mess and it smelled. He needed an upgrade urgently and the only way to do that was to get a pay rise from that skinflint, Fred.

He looked at the message icon. He could wait a bit longer for the generator to be fixed, maybe just long enough to see who had phoned. He pushed the screen and held it to his ear.

"Hi, I hope this is still Jim Crawley's number, if not just ignore this. Jim, it's Ben Night, you advised me on my book a few years back, well a lot of years back now, it was called Clownz and you pretty much told me everything you knew about the circus. I wondered if you had a few minutes to talk about the possibility of a bit more advice. I'll pay you for your time. Call me back."

Jim felt his eyes widen. This was it, this was where the big money came from. Last time, how long ago had that been? He had no idea, but there was a good pay cheque from Night, a very good pay cheque. But there should have been more. He'd been naïve and ignorant of the way things worked back then. He'd just been flattered that someone actually listened to him and not just stared like he belonged in a zoo. Back then, when Night came to the circus, none of the others wanted to talk to him, but Jim did. He didn't know much but he knew there might be a few quid in it for him.

He brought up the missed call and dialled Night back. He hardly ever read anything, not books anyway, but he bought ten copies of Clownz to give to anyone who showed an interest. He wasn't bothered about the story, he wanted everyone to see the dedication to him at the front. It said, 'Technical Advisor – Jim Crawley.'

Technical Advisor. It sounded impressive but nobody else thought it was. They just laughed and called him an idiot for not getting more money out of it. He had to agree on that score, he had missed out, so maybe now was the time for putting things straight.

"Hello?"

"Mr Night, it's me, Jim Crawley. Sorry I missed your call, I was in the middle of something."

"Hey, that's great. Bit of luck you still having the same number. How's tricks? How's the circus business treating you?"

Last time they spoke, Jim had lied about being a clown. Without actually being one, he knew almost everything there was to know about them. And when the time came for Night to watch a show, he'd 'fallen ill' that very evening and been unable to take part. What bad luck!

"Good, really good. Just finished a show actually. You said something about advising you again?"

No point in beating around the bush or making small

talk, he wanted to get down to business.

"Yes, so, I'm writing a new book with clowns in and I wanted to get some advice about a few things, you know, ensure it's authentic, like the last one. Reckon you can help?"

"No problem, no problem at all. As long as… well, I'm pretty busy at the moment, we're halfway through a run and then we'll be on the road again. I have to go where the money is, and there ain't that much of it about." There, just throw a few crumbs down for him to peck at.

"I'll pay you, Jim. I'll cover any lost earnings and I won't need that much help. I'm sure the circus business hasn't changed that much."

That was worrying. "We've had to move with the times, nothing stays the same. If you want your book to be up to date, we'll need more time than you might think." Nothing much had changed, except the costumes perhaps, but he needed to string this along for as long as he could.

"Okay, so what's the best way of doing this? You have access to email? I can write the questions up as I go and send them to you?"

Jim looked at the ancient, rusty fridge under the sink. He barely had electricity let alone Wi-Fi.

"No, my laptop's on the blink."

"Phone then?"

"We could but I can't guarantee I'll always be available. What about how we did it last time?" Meeting up would give him the chance to spin things out a little longer. It would also give him the opportunity to be a little more forceful with his request for more money. Just a little intimidating, perhaps.

"Meeting up? Where are you at the moment?"

Bingo. "For the next three days we're in some shit-hole called Matlock, in Derbyshire then we're…"

"Matlock? I can be there in twenty minutes."

He was keen. "It's late and I've only just finished. I can do tomorrow, that would be better." Keep him waiting just a little longer.

"Okay." He sounded disappointed. "What time?"

"Early as you like but I've got jobs to do at nine." Make it sound like you're not really bothered, that's the way to do it.

"I'll be there at seven?"

Jim could almost see the cash in his hand. "Great. My van is at the far end of the field, on its own." That was by design. Not his, by everyone else's.

"Brilliant, see you then."

Jim hung up. He could feel adrenalin pumping around his body. This was his chance to make some real money. This might be an opportunity to fix up the van, maybe even buy a new car. He didn't need to look in the mirror to know he was smiling. Possibilities were opening up again and he was buzzing.

Too wired, in fact, to bother about pretending to fix something that wasn't really broken. No, he needed another outlet for his energy. Something that would really tickle his funny bone. Half an hour with Denise while Fred's back was turned would not do the trick, not by a long chalk.

He reached into the cupboard above the sink and pulled out the clown mask. It was just a cheap one from a fancy dress shop. So cheap that instead of looking funny and friendly as he suspected it should, it looked deformed, ugly and scary as hell. That made it perfect.

The first time he'd used it had been with a prostitute years ago. Whether or not the police believed that she was raped was immaterial, the absolute bliss of the moment had stayed with him for weeks afterwards. The sex part of it was way down on the list. All he could think of, while he lay on top of her on that grubby mattress at the back of the shops, was what she was seeing. She had tried to close her eyes of course, but he'd told her if she did that, he would cut her throat open. So she saw a clown. An ugly, deformed and vile clown raping her.

The thought of it made him hard. There had been countless times since but none as powerful as that first time. Why would anyone believe them anyway? Most of them were so smacked up on dope that they could hardly think for themselves, let alone report it. He suspected not many of them reported being raped by a clown to the police. The cops would just tell them to go home and come down from whatever drug-fuelled fantasy they were in.

He pulled the mask on and took his favourite knife from the drawer. He knew just where to go. He'd been in this town before. He knew his way to the city, he knew where the streets were paved with girls just waiting for him to come. He whistled the old-time circus music and slipped his jacket on. Tonight was going to be a good night and tomorrow was already shaping into a fine day. Only good times lay ahead for Creepy Crawley.

He opened the caravan door and took the first step without looking ahead.

"Boo!"

Someone was outside his van – the voice made him jump. He felt his stomach lurch and he tried to step away, but his foot caught on the step and he fell back into the van. He closed his eyes as his head smashed into the toilet door, seeing only a bright burst of fireworks go off in his head.

"Boo!" the voice came again, before a boot heel came down on his clown mask and split his nose down the middle.

*

Jim rushed up through the misty oblivion and found that wherever he had just been was infinitely better than where he now was. It was dark, pitch black and he could taste blood. A lot of blood. He ran his tongue around his mouth and felt the jagged shards of smashed teeth shave the edges. He'd had some good beatings, his dad had been good at that before they took him away, but he'd always seen them coming. This was new, he'd been taken by surprise and someone had actually stamped on his head. His nose was smashed to pieces, he knew that; the pressure all across his swollen face was immense. It felt like his head would explode if it wasn't lanced.

He wasn't used to it. He was always the one in control. With the prostitutes, with Denise… ever since he was fifteen he had called the shots. People danced to his tune, whether they liked it or not. Usually not.

There was movement in the room with him, at the side

somewhere. He tried to move his head but couldn't, there was something across his head, neck and arms. He was tied down. He was lying flat on his back.

He opened his mouth to speak but something was gagging him. He whimpered. Was this revenge? Was it someone getting their own back on him for something he'd done? Maybe one of the smack-head girls had a pimp who wanted to teach him a lesson. He wanted to shout out, to tell them he would never do it again, that he had learned his lesson now and they could stop.

But he couldn't say anything. And he could hear someone moving about, walking slowly backwards and forwards. Their footsteps sounded hollow. He was still in the caravan which was good. They hadn't taken him anywhere to sort him out, they were going to do it right here.

Someone would hear and come to help. They would ignore the sign on the door that said, *'If it's rockin', don't come a knockin'* and rescue him from this sick bastard.

But his caravan was down at the bottom of the field, well away from the rest of the crew, just as he normally liked it. Nobody would hear him and if they did, they all hated him anyway. Was it one of them? Fred, perhaps? Panic flowered in his guts like a salmonella bug and sent a spasm all the way to his arse.

Don't shit yourself, Jimmy, they want you to do that so they can all laugh at you tomorrow. Creepy Crawley shit himself! Haha! Not a chance. He clenched his bum cheeks in defiance.

"Come on! Do your worst. Get on with it!" Those were

the words he formed in his head but all that came out was a long pathetic groan.

Then there was a silence, a stillness that told him someone was standing over him. They probably had a lump of wood, a bat or a pool ball inside a sock to beat him with. He tensed up and waiting for the real pummelling to start. Cowards. They couldn't take him in a fair fight so they were going to do it like this. He'd get them back, one day when they weren't watching.

But nothing happened for a while. Had they gone? Was it just a warning? He listened carefully. No, someone was still here, right above.

There was a sliver of light, then more and then…

Jim tried to scream but nothing came out. He tried to struggle but the bonds were too tight. It was a nightmare, a really bad nightmare and any minute he would wake up and it would all be over.

There was a clown staring down at him with most hideous snarl smeared across its face. It was the most frightening thing he had ever seen. Was this what the girls saw before Jim raped them? His bowels emptied and he groaned in disgust. The room hadn't been dark. It had been the mask he was wearing, the clown mask had been pushed to the side to blind him. He wanted it pushed back into place. He didn't want to see. He didn't want to see the clown that looked like the killer on the front of the book he had advised on. The book he had never read.

"Boo!" the clown whispered.

Creepy Crawley screamed his muffled cries for the next

hour as Sparkles's smile grew ever so slightly wider and his nose bloodier. The sign on Crawley's door, *'If it's rockin' don't come a knockin'* trembled as it had done hundreds of times over the years, and not one person took any notice of it.

11

Ben stood under the shower for a long time. His head was working at a million miles an hour but his body was still in the slow lane, the crawler lane behind an abnormal load. He hadn't slept again. Not because of the fever, which still gave him violent shivers, but because of the questions he was preparing for his meeting with Jim Crawley.

Now, as he stood in the shower, he could barely remember any of them. At least none of the questions he had thought were brilliant in the middle of the night. Maybe he should start keeping an ideas book beside the bed again. That really used to get Rachel in a knot. Flicking the light on at three in the morning to jot down some random thoughts that had just popped into his mind was not something she enjoyed. He tried to explain to her that if you wrote them down then you owned them, they couldn't fly away and or get stolen by another writer. But he could see she didn't really understand. At least not in the middle of the night.

As he got dressed for the first time in days, he realised how easy it would be not to get dressed ever again. He didn't have to get dressed to live a comfortable life. He could order shopping online, he could interact with other people online. He could even find sex online if he felt inclined to do so. It would be easy, it would be very easy, but it wouldn't do any sane person much good in the long run. He'd meet up with Jim, get some research done and then maybe take Stan for a walk in the Peak District. Maybe the fresh air would do both him and Stan some good.

He turned to the dog who was lying full stretch across the bed. "Go get your lead." Any mention of the word 'lead', whether it be in the right context or not, usually resulted in the same response. A whirling, whining, excited dog who rushed to the office door, where the lead was kept, and waited for Ben to come.

Stan lifted his head and pricked his ears. "Go on, go and get your lead." Stan whimpered and looked at the bedroom door. He didn't like to go anywhere in the house on his own now, not after their uninvited visitor had made an appearance. If it was at all possible, he stayed by Ben's side at all times. Toilet doors were no barrier either.

He scratched Stan behind the ear. Was it fear or was it his protective instinct that made him like that? Stan wasn't an aggressive dog. He didn't care for other dogs but he had never gone for one. As for people, well he loved just about everyone. Particularly if they scratched him behind the ear or gave him a biscuit.

How would he react if Ben was actually threatened?

Maybe Stan hadn't stood beside him the other night out of fear for himself, but to protect Ben.

"You don't need to worry about me, Stan The Man. He didn't want to hurt me, he was…" What was he doing? Being a muse? He shivered. "Trying to help me, that's all. Now come on, lets go meet a real clown." He stood up and felt the room tilt, his legs go to jelly. "Maybe I should eat something before we go."

He took the stairs very slowly with Stan on his heels.

*

Stan wasn't one for sitting in the boot. He never had been. He preferred the luxury of having the back seat to himself. The seatbelt buckles got in the way a bit but otherwise it was the perfect size for a greyhound to lie down and dream about dog things.

Stan sat up for the first part of the journey but it wasn't an easy fifteen minutes. The trickiest bit was reversing out of the garage. With Ben's shaky legs, controlling the clutch and accelerator pedals had been difficult and resulted in a jerking spasm across the drive. The wheel-spinning lurch up the track toward the village road did little to settle the dog either, but he carried on talking to Stan until the dog finally settled down onto the back seat with a grumpy grunt.

He accelerated through the village, gradually feeling more in control, and out onto the main road. It would only take about twenty minutes to get to the circus. As ill as he felt, he also felt excited. There were a lot of things about Jim Crawley that weren't straightforward but his motivation was clear as a bell. Money. That was it, pure and simple, he wanted money and lots of it. Ben didn't need to be a mind reader to work that out, nor to see that Crawley never had much money in his life.

It had been a while since they last talked. Crawley would have upgraded by now, but back then his caravan had been disgusting. There were photographs of half-naked models taped all over the walls and cigarette burns in all of the upholstery. Empty cans and dirty dishes in the sink completed the picture. Maybe he had a girlfriend or even a wife by now.

There was something *off* about the man though. Ben couldn't put his finger on it exactly but Jim Crawley didn't appear to have much of a sense of humour. He always found that surprising, given that his job was to make people laugh.

The only time Crawley laughed was at his own jokes, which weren't really jokes at all, they were vile two-liners about female anatomy. He doubted whether Crawley had ever read the book – if he had, he would have demanded more money, Ben was sure – but part of Sparkles had been based on Crawley. His laugh. Jim Crawley laughed like Muttley the dog and that was creepy, much like the nickname he probably didn't know he had.

However, he knew pretty much everything about how a circus worked and he knew absolutely everything there was to know about clowns. He had been one for most of his life. Ben needed that insight. You could research details on the internet and get a sense of things, but it was never the whole picture. No, that could only come from talking to people, being with them when they worked and listening to everything they said, not just when you were asking them questions. It was more important to listen to them conversing with their comrades and peers.

The signs for the circus started about two miles out of town. Above a picture of a clown with a wider smile than Sparkles ever had were the words 'Fred Ring-A-Ling's Circus is Back in Town!' It looked like someone had got excited at the printers because the letters were all in different colours. It was a good job he had dosed himself up to the gills before he left the house because the poster was trying to give him a migraine.

Ben pulled onto the memorial ground. Coming so early meant he missed all the commuter traffic, so it hadn't taken him as long to get here as he thought. The ground was all churned up, by both the weather and the number of vehicles that had driven over the grass in the last few days. Most of the caravans were bunched together to the side of the big top. The enormous tent's red and white stripes reminded him of the fevered nightmare he'd experienced a couple of nights before. The colours stood bright against what was otherwise a bleak scene. But one stood on its own, at the bottom of the field. It was a hundred metres from the others and he knew immediately that it was Jim's van. It didn't surprise him to see it was so far away from the rest.

He drove toward the van and saw Stan stand up in the back seat. He sniffed the air like he did in the days when Rachel cooked steak.

"Doubt you'll find much to eat where we're going, boy."

Only one or two of the other vans had lights on but Crawley's van was lit up against the bare trees behind it. The light wasn't strong, it looked like he had a low-watt bulb in a lamp. It looked grim. He pulled up beside the van and turned the engine off. The van looked to be the same as it was the last time they met. It might be a safer idea to take him for breakfast rather than risk stepping inside.

"We won't stay long, I promise." He climbed out and opened the door for Stan to charge from the car, but the dog sniffed the air again and sloped out slowly.

"Take your time, why don't you?" He took Stan's lead and the dog whined in reply.

It was probably just the smell of strange animals that made him reluctant to get out. There were elephants somewhere, and Stan wouldn't have smelled too many of them in his racing days.

They walked to the door, Ben reached up and banged on it. There was a sign on the door which wobbled as he knocked. He was about to read it when Stan pulled back away from the door. He whined again and backed away until the lead was taut.

"Don't be daft, come here." He tugged on the lead but Stan braced his powerful back legs. There was no way he was going to move. Ben felt too weary to get into a tug of war he knew he couldn't win.

"Go and have a wee then, but don't go far." He dropped the lead and banged on the door again.

"Jim, it's Ben Night, are you up?" He looked at Stan but the dog hadn't moved. He was still standing in the same spot. He made a long, low growl that made his jowls vibrate. Ben had never heard anything like it from him, or any other dog before.

"What's wrong with you? I'll take you to see the elephants in a minute and if they've got any tigers you can have a really close look at them too."

But Stan wasn't looking in the direction of the big top, or the woods. He was looking at the door handle. He was looking at it like he'd been looking at the clown the other night. Ben felt the hairs on the back of his neck stand on end, and shivered.

He reached up to knock again but Stan barked once. "Shut up, you'll wake everyone up!" Inside there was a feeling of dread winding its way through his stomach.

He looked at the door again. If Jim was in there then he would have heard him and answered the door, especially since he knew there was money in the offing. He looked over his shoulder at the rest of the site. Nobody was moving. It was dead.

The door handle was greasy and cold, as if it had been dipped in oil. It moved down easily and the door swung open.

"Jim, are you there, mate?" A smell rushed out of the van. A smell of stale cigarette smoke, of alcohol, of grease and something else too. It was the smell of a butcher's shop.

Stan whined softly but he was back at his side again. Ben took the first step and then the second before he could see inside. He craned his neck but it was gloomy and the only lamp seemed to throw a filthy stain around the interior. A dirty old fridge obscured his view down the van but there was shape on the bed. A big lumpy shape. Maybe he was just drunk. He felt slightly reassured that someone was home.

"Jim?" No reply and no movement. "It's me. It's Ben."

He took the final step into the caravan and heard Stan's paws ring on the metal step below. The dog was following him. Was it a good idea to wake Crawley up, to shove him and disturb his rest? He should just leave and come back tomorrow morning. Waking a man with a bad hangover was never…

As his eyes adjusted to the gloom he saw dark stains on the bed, huge dark stains, and on the walls there were more dark stains. Great arcs of liquid had been sprayed up the walls and onto the tacky posters. He lifted his head. There were the same spatters of liquid on the ceiling too and the lamp shade was dark but not by design, but the coating on it. A thick, congealed coating of blood.

Nausea swept over him immediately, nearly knocking him off his feet, but as he looked away his eyes settled on the floor. There were letters written in blood.

"Boo!" he whispered and his vision closed in at the sides. Sweat dripped into his eyes and he retched.

"Back, Stan, ba…" And then the scene was gone and Stan was yelping as he fell onto him, onto the metal steps. Blackness.

*

It was the screaming that brought him back to the world. The piercing shrieks of someone who saw what he had just seen. He felt sick again. The stink of butchered meat was still in his nostrils. But it wasn't pig, cow or lamb, it was human. It was Jim Crawley.

Ben rolled onto his side and vomited. It made his eyes water, both with the strength of the heave and the acid clawing at his fragile throat. He winced and wiped his mouth.

"Police, someone call the police!" a woman's voice shouted.

Stan. Where was Stan? He rolled over and looked at the van. The dog was lying down next to him, panting and watching people running across the field toward them. A lone woman was standing in the door to the caravan, just where he had stood, with her hands over her mouth. She looked down at Ben with wide-eyed horror. And then her eyes narrowed and there was another emotion in there too. Fury.

She jumped down the steps and stood over him. "You! You did this!" She spat the words at him.

"What? No! I found him. I found him like that!" His throat burned and his voice sounded like a whisper although he was shouting.

A man charged up the steps and stood motionless at the top. It looked like he was about to take another step but he looked down, stopped and tilted his head to read what had been written in Crawley's blood.

A second woman stood on the steps behind him. "What is it? What's happened to him?" She was craning her neck to look in but the man blocked her view.

The woman standing over Ben turned to them. "He did it! I've got him here." Stan whined and pawed at Ben's arm. He didn't like how things were panning out. Neither did Ben.

"I didn't do anything!" he shouted. "I found him, for god's sake!" He tried to stand up but his legs felt like they were made of custard, and when he moved an explosion of pain erupted in his head. If he'd felt ill this morning, he felt like death right now.

The man in the caravan pushed past the woman and stood over Ben. He had the most perfectly clipped handlebar moustache he had ever seen. He looked like a strongman from a Victorian circus.

He twisted his head, looked Ben up and down. "I doubt it." He looked at the woman. "This is that writer. Look at his clothes. Whoever did that would be covered in Creepy's blood. Go and make sure someone's called the rozzers."

She opened her mouth to reply, but seemed to realise it was futile and sprinted back up the field.

"Nice dog you've got there, Mr Night. Racer, is he?" He offered his hand and Ben took it to pull himself upright. The friendly nature of his greeting and the normality of the conversation was almost as shocking as finding Crawley.

"Was. He's retired now." Ben smoothed Stan's head. "And yes, he is a good dog." His head was swimming and his vision was blurred at the edges.

"You look like you need a cup of tea. Come on, I'll take you up to my van." He looked at Crawley's van. "We'll let the police sort that out. Good riddance, I say."

Ben was shocked by the remark, but he let the other man take him by the elbow and lead him away. He clutched Stan's lead tightly in his hand. As they walked toward the other caravans, he could already hear the sound of sirens in the distance.

"Thanks," Ben said. "I thought I was going to get lynched back there."

"There's not many folk who care whether Jim Crawley's dead or alive. You were just unlucky, that woman happens to be one of them."

He helped Ben inside the van, which was more like a house than a caravan. The woman who had accused him was sitting on the sofa with the phone in her hands. She eyed Ben as he walked in.

"You've met my wife, Denise. Whoever did that to Creepy saved me a job. Sooner or later I'd have done it myself." He switched the kettle on. "Tea?" He smiled.

Ben nodded.

Half an hour later there was a knock at the door. Fred Ring opened the door to a young-looking detective. Immediately, his appearance gave Ben the impression that this was going to be a different approach to the one by DC Kelly.

The officer was slow and methodical, taking down every detail about Ben's association with Crawley: how he had made contact with him, what Crawley was like on the phone and his route to the circus that morning. He made fastidious notes, pausing only to clarify a detail Ben felt was minor. By the time he was describing how he found Crawley in the caravan, he felt exhausted and his headache had grown into a whopper.

The detective offered to call an ambulance but Ben refused. He had been unconscious but only for a few seconds. If he was made to wait at accident and emergency, it would only make things worse.

After he told the officer everything he expected to be able to go, but the detective went on to write it all out again in front of him. As he read the long version back, Ben was astounded by the level of detail. Some of it he thought was inconsequential unless…

"Am I a suspect?" He signed the last sheet on the statement and handed it back.

The detective opened his mouth but as he did, a call came through on his radio which he answered. It might have been his imagination but Ben thought he looked relieved not to have to answer the question.

"On my way." The officer ended the call and stood up. "You're free to go now, Mr Night, we'll be in touch." He started walking out and Ben followed behind with Stan. He opened and closed his mouth several times. Did he want to ask that question again? Why would he be a suspect he hadn't done anything wrong?

He walked down the steps and walked across the field to his car. As he got closer, he could see how many people were buzzing around the caravan. Blue and white striped tape had been secured around two trees to contain the scene. Unfortunately his car was inside the cordon.

He approached it and asked an officer in uniform if he could get his car.

"I'll check," he said and spoke to someone on his radio. He turned his back to Ben as if that would stop him hearing the conversation.

After a second he turned back around. "Someone's coming to talk to you."

Ben sighed. All he wanted was to get back home and crawl into bed. He wanted to sleep, forget what he'd seen and what it meant. He would think about that tomorrow when the pain in his head wasn't quite so crippling.

"Mr Night?"

He turned. A petite woman with flame-red hair scraped back from her face stood in front of him. She reached down and stroked Stan.

"I need my car back, please," he said.

She winced. "I'm really sorry but we need to keep it here for a few more hours." She was attractive, and her blue eyes never left his. It was disarming.

"For how long?" he asked.

"I'll give you a lift home. It's not too far, is it." It wasn't a question, she clearly knew exactly where he lived. "Then when we're finished with it, we'll drop it off. Okay?"

"Finished with it? What are you going to do to it?" He looked past her. A man in a white suit was already looking around the car.

"It's in the middle of a murder scene, Mr Night." As if that was all she needed to say to answer his question. "Have you got your keys handy?"

He reached into his pocket and handed them over. She tossed them to the white-suited man by his car.

"My car's up there." She pointed toward the big top. "Come on, I'll take you home, you look and sound like you need a lie down." She turned and looked at a tall, bald man who was busy writing something into a large pink book. "Just taking Mr Night home, boss."

The Boss held his hand up without lifting his head.

"I'm Jane Brady, by the way." She started walking away from the caravan. Ben took one last look at his car and the caravan, then followed her.

"Well, you know who I am and this is Stan."

Whoever Jane Brady was, she wasn't just another detective. She had an air of someone who was more in charge than The Boss, whoever he was, would ever be.

"Did anyone take your fingerprints or a sample of your DNA yet?" she asked casually.

"No," he answered. He was a suspect then.

"No problem, I'll do it when we get to your place. We just need to make sure we know who's been inside Mr Crawley's van." She paused as if hearing his thoughts. "So we can eliminate them from the enquiry."

"Right," Ben replied. He felt sick again. Very, very sick.

12

Jane hadn't offered to take Night home out of kindness. No, it was an excellent opportunity to spend some time with the man. A chance to speak to him and find out what he was like. The evidence would prove whether he was involved or not, but finely honed instinct told her he wasn't. Officers were already accessing all of the CCTV cameras on his route to see if his story was true. And if it was, there was still a connection between him and the three murders. How did that link work? That was the question.

The forensics team should have taken his samples and she should have kept him at the scene to complete that task, but taking them at his house was another opportunity too good to miss.

Sparkles was his creation. The mutilated paedophile, Newman, had used that creation to further his own vile crimes. He was acquainted with Night too. The author told Stu that he'd signed thousands of books and had no idea who Harvey Newman was. Plausible.

Stu had spoken to him about the murder and had not been impressed with the man. That fact alone didn't make him a bad guy. Stu tended to rub most people up the wrong way and reactions to him were usually negative.

And then there was Crawley and all that blood. She had never seen that much blood before or in such spectacular patterns all over the interior. It meant he was alive when he was carved up. At least through part of it anyway.

The clown mask Crawley wore had been stabbed so many times that it had sunk into the spongy flesh beneath and had to be pulled off his face. Beneath the mask was nothing more than a ruined lump, parts of which had been cut away. The killer had also paid attention to his hands and cock. Both of which had been hacked off and thrown on the floor, unlike parts of his face which had been taken away again. It was horrific, it was a bloodbath and her initial reaction had been to run outside and throw her guts up into the woods, but she hadn't. She had parked her revulsion to one side and considered her options, considered her strategy and how she would brief DI White.

On the surface, it looked like a frenzied attack. That was unlike the other two where it seemed the mutilation had been more deliberate. More care had been taken to remove the face, rather than stab the hell out of it. The word written at the scene, in the victim's blood, was always the same though. That never changed.

Night was surly in the car on the way back. But no more than the average man who had just lost his car and was suffering from a cold. She hadn't learned anything she couldn't have found in an internet search, and she wasn't familiar enough with his books to try and massage his ego. So she made do with small talk about the dog.

He evidently loved the dog and the sentiment appeared to be reciprocated.

She knew from the file that Night was within a year of her age and divorced. His house was beautiful from the outside, the surrounding fields giving it a wonderfully remote feel. She hadn't gone farther than the hallway but the house looked big enough for a family of ten to live there, in some comfort.

When Jane returned to the station, she immediately went online and ordered six of his books for her Kindle. She knew it was good research and it might make a refreshing change from the crap she normally read.

DI White poked his head out of his office. "Jane, you got a minute?"

He was already back at the station by the time she returned, but had been on the telephone for almost the entire time, intermittently jabbering away followed by a prolonged period of silence. By the sound of it, he was speaking to someone above him in the command chain.

She walked into his office.

"Shut the door a minute." He took a deep breath as if he was about to deliver some bad news. "And take a seat."

Jane did as she was asked.

"Hargreaves has been told by the command team to bring someone in."

This is what always happened. The chief got tense if nobody

was arrested within a week. Appearing in front of the press to tell them that they had a suspect in custody made everyone happier, including the public. Even if it wasn't the right person.

"Who do you suggest?" She wanted to get someone locked up too. But only if it was the right person.

"What about Night? He's the only link to all three we've got at the moment."

She had considered the very same thing, and even thought about her grounds for arresting him when she was at his house. They were flimsy at best. If they brought him in, the media circus would be incredible. Above all, having spent an hour with him, she knew someone else was behind the killings. She might be wrong but her gut told her Ben Night didn't have it in him to punch anyone, let alone mutilate someone like that.

"Yes there's a link, but that link is going to identify the killer." She paused then added "It's not him."

He undid his top button and loosened his tie. "We need to get someone in and soon."

"I appreciate that but it needs to be the right person." She wouldn't be pressured into an arrest just for the sake if it. "Look boss, it's not like the trail has gone cold, is it? We've got three scenes now, three chances to get something from forensics." She could see this didn't appease him. "If Night's car doesn't show on the CCTV trawl then maybe we can think again about fetching him in."

"You've got someone on it?"

"Bilby and Morris are both on it. Should be finished before end of play today."

"Good. What do you need from me? I've got to ring him back in half and hour."

Stu's murder was still with the other team but her squad had now picked up Crawley's murder as well as Newman's. She was running out of staff.

"Bodies. I need more bodies. As many as you can get."

He jotted it down. "Anything else? What about surveillance on Night?"

She shook her head. "Not yet. We will need him though. He's our key and he probably knows more than he thinks he does."

"Okay." He dropped his pen. "What about you?"

This was it, the dreaded welfare check. "I'm fine. It's frantic but that's how I like it. Keeps me out of trouble."

He nodded and stifled a yawn. "Frantic isn't the word."

Jane smiled and stood up. "I'll let you know how the CCTV goes."

"Please."

She walked back to her desk and sat down. This was White's first murder investigation and he looked dreadful. Maybe she should have asked him how *he* was. But it wasn't her place, that was Hargreaves's job. She doubted any of them were doing very well.

She got comfortable and started working through the new tasks generated by HOLMES. The system was supposed to be foolproof, wouldn't miss a trick. She had to agree it was superb for recording all enquiries, the officers assigned to them and the results. But sometimes it was too prescriptive, too regimented and removed the good old-fashioned gut feeling. Nevertheless it was the system she had to use and it generated hundreds of tasks which had to be allocated.

She looked around the office. It was more or less empty. Jane felt bad at having to dish out yet more jobs to them all. She needed bodies, lots and lots of bodies.

At just after ten o'clock that night, her phone rang. It was Nicky Morris, one of the officers on the CCTV trawl.

"We've got him driving through Matlock at six-fifty this morning. The cameras follow him all the way through."

So Night's story checked out. Jane felt vindicated by her decision not to arrest him.

Morris continued "No sign of him last night either. The circus finished at ten and the roads were busy then but by half-past it was dead again. Typical Thursday night in the sticks."

That news further justified her feelings about him. Morris sounded excited, as if she was bursting to reveal something she had been holding back.

"But…" She paused. "You might be interested in this."

A box at the bottom of Jane's screen told her an email had just arrived from Nicky Morris, who was now whistling the creepy circus music she hated. It sounded eerie and distorted down the telephone line, making her wince.

"You can't hold a tune, Nicky."

Jane opened the message. A grainy image opened up on the screen and below it were four others. Together they formed a sequence showing the movement of a vehicle across the front of a petrol station. Jane stared at the screen and felt her heart rate increase two-fold. Although the image was poor in quality, she knew what it was immediately.

Bingo The Clown was on the move again.

The images showed him from the side. As she looked at them the screen flickered, making his smile seem to move, to twitch in front of her and grow in size. She would have to check but on the image she found after Stu had been killed, she was sure his distorted grin was just under his cheeks. Now it looked as if it was an inch or two higher. Maybe it was an optical illusion or her tired mind giving it properties it didn't possess. His face was so white too, ghostly white, which she shouldn't be surprised about since this was the driving, murdering ghost of Harvey Newman. Perhaps…

"Have you seen the window?" Morris asked.

Jane had been staring so intensely at the driver that she hadn't seen anything else. She shifted her focus to the front passenger window which was closest to the camera. Just under his head and in dark letters was a single word. One they had all seen too many times in the last week.

"Boo!" she said. "He knows we can see him. He knows and he's enjoying it." The letters weren't all recognisable and the exclamation mark ran down the inside like it was wet. She knew it was blood. Jim Crawley's blood.

Morris sounded deflated as she gave the next update. "We've gone through all the footage but the number plate is unreadable on all of them. It's probably nicked anyway. Looks another old one though."

It was an old car shape, Eighties or Nineties at a push. They were easy to steal. They rarely had alarms or immobilisers, and the old-style ignitions were easy to bypass.

"Thanks, Nicky. Listen, you and Andy get off home. Fast-track has all been done so we'll start again in the morning."

She examined the images again, looking for something that would give him away. There was nothing. She called White over to look at it but he couldn't see anything that would help them either.

All he said was, "He's driving in the direction of Night's house."

And he was, but that road also linked up with any number of major routes as well as the M1.

They walked across the car park together. White looked even worse than he had earlier. He was hunched over, twisted, limping on his left leg.

"You okay?" she asked despite not wanting to earlier. She couldn't ignore how bad he looked now they were walking together.

"My back's killing me." He added quickly "I'll be fine, I just need to lie down." His car indicators flashed twice in the darkness.

"Goodnight." Jane started walking to her own car but was stopped by a hand on her arm.

"We're not missing anything, are we?" White asked.

She looked into his eyes. He looked stressed and tired. It was a bad combination, particularly when that tiredness would be relentless for several more weeks.

"Nothing. HOLMES won't let us miss anything. We'll get him, boss. It's just a matter of time."

"We will, I know we will but how many more will he… will he do what he did to Crawley. That was sickening." He paused and seemed to consider his words carefully. "Depraved that a human being would do that to…"

He let go of her arm and smiled. "Time for a beer I think, a beer and a lie down."

Jane laughed but it felt uneasy, like laughing at a funeral. White was struggling, both physically and mentally, that much was clear. He looked lost just then, completely lost at sea. He would have seen some grim sights in Social Services but nothing could prepare anyone for the bloodbath in Crawley's caravan. What could ever prepare a person for that?

*

She opened a bottle of beer and climbed into bed. It was too late to lie in the bath for hours getting all wrinkly, so she had showered and put her pyjamas on. She stared at the cover of her paperback book. It was a piece of Regency romanticism that was about as far away from police work as you could hope to get. It was also crap of the highest order.

She put her iPad on and opened the Kindle app. The Ben Night books she downloaded earlier appeared on the carousel, so she turned them one at a time to look at the covers. She knew which one she wanted to read, it was the obvious choice, but needed to see what the others were like.

A vampire, a werewolf, a zombie, a demon, a man and finally a clown were all placed carefully against a plain black background. That gave Night his brand. The most effective one by far was Clownz. Maybe it was because the clown looked a lot like Harvey Newman's clown. No, it was more likely Newman had made his clown look like the character in Night's book. With a few subtle changes like removing the sharpened teeth and the crazy eyes, that would just scare the kids before he had a chance to take away their innocence. The make-up was similar though, particularly the diamonds around the eyes and the smile. She supposed most clowns had enormous smiles, but both the cover and the CCTV footage showed a clown with a grotesquely proportioned grimace.

She opened the book and started reading. The sight of Crawley's caravan had obviously disturbed White. To a lesser extent, she had also been affected by it. If you weren't then you had no place in society, or the job, but how was Night coping with it? Did his writing or his research prepare him for a horrific sight like that?

After the first chapter, reading his blood-curdling descriptions, she knew he either had an extremely vivid imagination or had seen a human getting butchered. She was also hooked.

*

The following morning, just as she was getting dressed, her mobile rang.

"DS Brady." She used her shoulder to hold it to her ear while she continued buttoning up her blouse. She had woken up feeling groggy, as if she drank more than just the two bottles of beer. It could easily have been more if she hadn't put the brakes on. She hadn't wanted to stop reading, but at gone one o'clock knew she needed to get some sleep.

She recognised White's voice. "We've found the car, or at least what's left of it."

Her spirits sank. "Burnt out?"

"Afraid so. I got a call about fifteen minutes ago. Meet me there?"

"Where?" She picked up her car keys and walked quickly downstairs.

"The flats on High-Bank."

White ended the call just as Jane reached the front door. She paused for a moment, turned and walked back to the kitchen. She would need some medication if she was going to be on top of her game today. Plenty of it too.

Had she caught flu from Night? She hoped not, she hadn't even had the pay-off of kissing him to get it.

13

Maldon heard the sirens long before the pulsing blue light whirled across the ceiling above his bed. It could only mean they'd found his car.

He had travelled around the country in stolen cars before. The trick was never to keep one for too long, keep changing them every few days. He knew not to leave any evidence at all. Cigarette butts, chewing gum, hair fibres and fingerprints were all likely to get you arrested. The only sure way to avoid leaving anything was to burn the car after you'd finished with it.

Torching it behind the flats had been risky, but he knew there was no CCTV covering either the car park or the street. And all the other residents were either drugged up, pissed up, or out burgling houses. It was either that or walk around the streets having Sparkles screaming at him to hide every few seconds. Sparkles was probably right though. Just looking as he did was apt to get him arrested.

Sparkles had told him to write 'Boo!' on the car window

in blood. That had been a good idea too. He didn't half go on sometimes but he also had some brilliant ideas, particularly when it came to killing people. Especially when it came to the clown living in the caravan.

In the darkness, the fire had burned so bright that it hurt his eyes to look at it. Sparkles had squealed in delight as the flames reached out and licked the air.

"Look what we've done. It's like all the Guy Fawkes bonfires you missed, all rolled into one!"

And Sparkles was right about that too. He was sure his parents must have had fireworks when he was little, he was just too young to remember them. But this made up for all the missed parties. There was even a mini-explosion at one point, making him step back from the window.

"Don't be such a scaredy-cat, Mouldy! Just enjoy it!"

He had enjoyed it, right up to the point where the fire engine arrived and put the fire out. Of course, by then the car was just a charred skeleton and the fire was dying down, but it had been disappointing just the same.

"Rotters!" Sparkles shrieked at them through the window.

"Shh, they'll hear you!" Maldon took a step away from the window. Sparkles laughed then, like he always did.

"I wonder if his head reaches right to the top of that helmet? If we cut it off we could have a look." Sparkles really laughed then, and Maldon had to admit it was an infectious and pleasant sound. Relaxed, he went back to the window to watch the display for a while; to slip into a daydream about a lost childhood and listen to the carnival music.

He got up from the bed as the police arrived, in cars with

flashing blue lights. He didn't understand that. There was no emergency, the car was just a scorched skeleton, so what was the rush? Then an unmarked car arrived and a woman with hair the same colour as the flames got out. She put her hands on her hips and started talking to the fireman with the white helmet. Maldon watched two of the other firemen nudge each other, looking her up and down. Another man appeared, a tall man with a bald head. They all talked to each other as if they were discussing some conspiracy.

There was something about that tall man. Something he… They all started looking around at the houses and flats. He stepped back before they saw him.

"You're just a face at the window, Maldon, they won't recognise you. Stick two fingers up at them, go on!"

Maldon wasn't so sure it was a good idea. Police officers were usually pretty good at recognising people, especially clowns.

That was the entertainment over for the day and he fell onto his bed feeling disappointed. The little record player in the back of his brain was only halfway through the carnival tune but he moved the needle to the start and tuned into it. The music played all the time, on a constant loop. It was beautiful in an off-key, creepy way.

When he had trouble sleeping he started the music from the beginning, because that was his favourite part, and turned it up. It didn't disturb him, quite the contrary, it was like the lullabies he imagined he might have listened to as a child. Within a few seconds of the music starting, he was immediately transported to a world where he was that child again.

There was the most enormous red and white striped big top ever. It was decorated in a million golden light bulbs which threw a warming glow all over his little face. He pushed through the great flapping canvas door, saw the huge sawdust-covered circle and rows of seats stretching into the darkness at the top of the tent. The seats were completely empty, not another single person was allowed inside. It was for him and him alone.

The ring was covered in fresh, untouched sawdust. This was where all the acts would perform. The fierce lions and their trainers, the powerful strongman, the majestic acrobats and maybe a single white horse with a beautiful lady standing on its back. Then of course there would be the clowns, his absolute favourite!

The tent was so vast that he could barely see what act had already come out, but he could hear the wonderful music, the wonderful Entry of the Gladiators being played perfectly on an organ. He walked toward it, the sweet smells of candyfloss and popcorn tickling his nostrils. Then there was the delicious aroma of hotdogs and fried onions which made his mouth water. Oh, how he wished he could have enjoyed this moment with his mum and dad.

But this was no time for melancholy thoughts, this was a time to be happy, to enjoy the circus! He ran toward the ring, toward the enormous organ that was somehow playing itself in the centre. What sort of an instrument could do that? Was it magic? The music was more delicious than the candyfloss, hotdogs and popcorn together. It *was* magic.

His legs started to tire but he wasn't going to give up

before he got there, no matter how out of breath he was. Louder and louder it grew, and he could almost see the pretty little notes floating into the air. The clowns would be there, the clowns with their funny shoes, red noses and lovely wide smiles, would transport him to another place. A happier place.

As he skidded in the sawdust and stopped at the barrier, he saw that the organ stretched into the darkness above his head. The pipes were not shiny and golden as he had imagined they would be. No, they were covered in thick, black oil and some of the enormous keys were missing. And now he knew why it was so badly out of tune.

Where were the clowns? They should be here to welcome him, they should be…

A hot and sour breath whispered down the back of his neck. "Boo!"

*

Maldon jerked into life and sat upright.

"They're here. They've come to get us," Sparkles whispered.

The room was light now, but he had no idea how long he had been asleep.

"Who?" he whispered back.

"You'll see," Sparkles replied.

Maldon lay still for a minute but there was nothing. Maybe Sparkles was wrong this time. He was about to get up when there was a loud banging on the door.

"Told you!"

"Should I answer it?" he whispered.

"Doh! Who do you think it is?"

He didn't need to answer that. It was the police, it had to be.

"Hello!" He heard a voice shout from outside.

"Just lie still and they'll go away," Sparkles instructed him.

He did as he was told and held his breath too, just for good measure. He could hear doors being knocked all the way up the road. They were checking house-to-house to see if anyone had seen the car getting torched. They wouldn't get much joy down here and even less luck in the flats. He heard his letter box open and close. It would be a note asking him to ring in.

"You should ring them, just for the giggles!" Sparkles spoke loudly now, confident that the police had left. He might have to think about that one, he wasn't sure if it was such a good idea.

He rolled out of bed and went to find something to eat. There wasn't much to get excited about, but there was a box of Frosties which he took to his computer and ate dry straight out of the box. They were stale and tasted woody but at least it was something to put in his aching belly.

He put the box down, wiped his sticky fingers over his legs. The sensation was unpleasant and spiky. His fingers had rubbed against something crusty. He was still wearing the overalls he'd worn to kill the copper and the caravan clown. They were smeared in dried blood and bits of… well, bits of human.

He shrugged, licked his fingers and looked up. His eyes caught the creased, stained photograph he kept stuck on the edge of the monitor. It was the only possession he had to remind him how Mum and Dad looked, and he only had that because it was in his hand when they took him away from the house. The colours had faded so almost everyone looked like they had a bad case of jaundice. He had no idea when or where it was taken. Nobody was smiling in the photograph. In fact Dad was looking away and he looked angry. Maldon liked to imagine that just off camera were a group of coppers coming to arrest him and he was shouting, *"You'll never take me alive!"* or something like that.

Even though she was his mum, Maldon thought she was ugly. She was fat and looked like she had a bad taste in her mouth. Over the years he had imagined having hundreds of rows with both of them about all manner of things, both trivial and not. After all, that was what happened in families wasn't it?

It was twenty years since the clown had killed Mum and Dad. It had taken as long as that for him to come back to the county. His support worker didn't think it was a good idea at first. But Maldon had been persuasive, and in the end the worker thought it was such a terrific idea that he found him a house to rent. Getting Maldon off the drugs was his 'top priority' and getting him away from his circle of 'criminal friends' had been his 'ultimate goal.' If that meant coming here then that's what it took. Maldon knew about the cross-dressing prostitute his support worker visited and that helped persuade him too.

He hunched over the keyboard and started writing the back story of the circus worker. How he came to work in the circus, what he liked to do when he wasn't working. It would end in his gruesome murder, they always did, but it was good to start a new story. There was a twinge of sadness as he started typing, the circus music slowing in tempo. The story was nearing its conclusion, and soon it would end. His smile hadn't returned, although he had felt several tickling sensations at the corners of his mouth when he slaughtered the circus worker. It was trying to come through, that was for sure, so he shouldn't get too disheartened. There were still a few chapters left to go and the ending was still to be worked out, so there was plenty of time.

His fingers moved quickly over the keys. He was getting faster at typing and it helped that Sparkles was dictating the story to him. He was allowed to add his own flourishes occasionally but mostly Sparkles was the creative one. Except when it came to killing, then he was the artist.

He needed to work quickly today too. Tonight he had a couple of visits to make.

*

He didn't have to walk far before finding a suitable car. The police had long since left the area and a lorry took the burned-out wreckage away. He walked through the dark streets with his hoodie pulled tight around his face. Even that hadn't been enough for Sparkles.

"Hurry!" he squealed. *"Hurry, hurry, hurry!"*

It made him nervous and the coat hanger got jammed as he tried to lift the door lock. He didn't like doing it but was forced to growl at Sparkles to shut him up. After that,

BOO!

opening and starting the Vauxhall had been easier.

This car was particularly bad. Its engine sounded like it belonged in a tractor and it didn't go much above thirty-five miles an hour. As long as it didn't draw too much attention to him, he would be fine. He had a visit to make before he went to see Mr Night. A visit to his past. One he had been putting off ever since he came back.

He drove past the entrance to the cul-de-sac three times before he dared turn in. Each time he didn't have the stomach to look down into it, he just drove straight past as if he were on the way somewhere else, somewhere he needed to be. And each time he sat shaking at the junction a hundred metres away, shaking and feeling sick. All the time Sparkles had been silent and so had the music.

On the last occasion, he actually started crying as he neared the turning for Wilson Croft. The tears ran from his eyes and were gobbled up under the mask by Sparkles immediately. He had no time for tears. It was smiles all the way. But as the tears leaked he could feel the smile on Sparkles's face dropping, inch by miserable inch. All his good work was being undone.

He stopped the car opposite number 12 and turned off the engine. Everything was completely silent for the first time in a very long time. He wished Sparkles would shout at him, would tell him off for crying like a baby, but he didn't utter a sound.

Maldon couldn't turn his head to look at the house for a very long time. He knew the longer he sat there, the more chance there was of someone spotting him. He was in a cul-de-sac at one in the morning, after all.

The last time he was here was when they took him out of the house. There were people everywhere; police officers in uniform and some in suits and people he now knew were from Social Services. Men and women with comforting smiles who smelled of Polo mints and perfume.

They made him take off his pyjamas and push them straight into a long brown bag. One of the officers had scribbled something on the outside of the bag and stacked it with the others. He still remembered the design on the pyjamas too. They were special ones with oriental symbols stitched into the fabric. He had no idea what the markings said but Dad had told him they were magic words and could teach him how to do kung fu in his sleep.

They were ruined though. The material was soaked in blood – in Mum and Dad's blood – so there was no way he could ever wear them again. He cried when they took him out of the house. Not just cried but wailed and screamed. He remembered how it had all seemed like a dream, like a nightmare, a really bad nightmare.

He turned slowly and looked at the house that had been his home for the first nine years of his life. Part of it was illuminated by the street light, throwing an orange glow across the front room window. It made the house look sick and it matched the feeling in his stomach. The front room had been painted a pale yellow colour which always seemed to look dirty, and there was a television in one corner.

He had watched Dad punch Mum in the face, knocking her into the television in that room. Dad had bought a new TV because Mum knocked the old one over as she fell. It made the screen smash. On sunny days, if the cartoons were boring he would look at the wall behind the television and see the faint bloodstain from Mum's nose when it exploded. The stain was always there, no matter how many times they painted over it. Or maybe it was his imagination?

After twenty-one years, the act of picturing the inside of the house was tricky. He had spent only one third of his life in that house, and things that had happened since were easier to recall. Things that lay on top of old memories and pushed them down deeper in his mind. He remembered his room, although he couldn't be sure what colour it was, or what his favourite toy had been. He didn't really remember the garden either, although he was sure there was one. The bathroom and the dining room were also complete blanks.

But he couldn't forget the kitchen. Nor could he forget the way Dad's head lolled to the side with the insides of his throat on show. Or the look in his mother's eyes as the blade disappeared into her neck. There had been so much blood too. Much more than at the clown's house or the copper's or in the caravan, even though they had been mutilated much worse.

But he supposed there had been two people in the kitchen with their throats cut. Two people's blood up the walls, on the ceiling, on the cooker and coating the door of the glossy white fridge-freezer in fat, red rivers. The whiteness of the fridge look how a bone looked through a deep cut through the flesh.

What happened after they took him from the house had lasted for twenty-one years. It was still happening to him, and because of that it was far worse than the bloodbath. The examination of his body, the interviews, being asked to go over and over and over the same thing time and time again had all been nauseating. Describing the clown and how he did what he did to Mum and Dad, reliving the horror over a hundred times, had been more than his immature mind was able to cope with. The police officers, the care workers, the counsellors, the drugs, the breakdowns, all of it as a result of the clown and what he did. All of it.

He reached over and grabbed the filthy knife from his bag. He was going to cut Sparkles out of his life for good. The tip of the knife pressed against his cheek, puncturing through the layer of Sparkles's mask.

"No, no, no!" the clown squealed. *"Kill me and you'll never get it back. I'm the only one who can help you, silly boy!"*

Maldon held the knife in place for a moment and then threw it back into the bag.

"It wasn't me, it was Bingo, the one you carved up. Remember?"

Maldon was confused and his head, face and body ached with each beat of his heart. He stripped off his gloves and worked his teeth around what was left of his fingernails. In the past he always reached for drugs to smooth away the anxiety, to help him cope with the anger, frustration and confusion. But he wouldn't do that again. It would render him incapable of doing what he needed to do. He looked at the tips of his fingers. None of them had nails he could bite any longer and they all stung horribly. Nevertheless they would just have to do until the story was finished and the last word typed. He slipped the gloves back on, wincing as he pulled them tight over his fingertips.

He took one last look at the house then started the car again. The next chapter was on the seat beside him and he needed to deliver it to Ben.

14

After the detective left, Ben locked both the front and back doors. Then he went from room to room, checking all of the windows. Stan stayed by his side throughout, not at Ben's request but of the dog's own volition. Stan had an almost permanent look of anxiety on his face. It was as if he expected the worst to happen at any time. That look seemed to have grown deeper and darker in the last few days.

He shouldn't give the dog human expressions and feelings, he knew that, but the way Stan felt the need to touch him almost constantly was a sign of fear and protection. It was a simple reaction, not singularly human or canine. It was pack mentality; protection in numbers. Whatever it meant, it was comforting for both of them.

When he was satisfied the house was totally secure, he checked the internet for an alarm company and called them. There was room on his credit card to have one fitted but even after pleading with several companies to come that same day, none could manage it and he had to settle for nearly a week later.

He double-checked the doors and windows again, with Stan for company, and took a mug of hot lemon to bed. Stan led the way up the stairs but Ben had to keep nudging him with his knee to keep the dog moving. Every two steps, the dog paused and sniffed at the air. Whatever he was sniffing at was well out of Ben's range but it was unnerving all the same.

He put the mug down and groaned as he fell onto the bed. The adrenalin rush he had felt rushing through his body last night and this morning had gone completely. The buzzing ideas about his book were lying wingless and dead at the base of his brain now, and in their place were pictures of a grotesque clown butchering Jim Crawley's face. He felt only the slightest twinge of grief for Crawley. He barely knew the man and what he did know wasn't particularly good, but nobody deserved to be treated like that.

Stan whimpered at the side of him, as if he too was disturbed by the same thoughts. Ben put his hand down and smoothed the silky soft fur on the dog's head.

"Reckon I should've told her about the manuscript?" He didn't look at Stan but he could feel his eyes on him.

"Yep, you're right as usual."

There was no doubt about it, he should have told Brady about the night-time deliveries. Apart from today, he never had much to do with the police. The books he wrote seldom involved the law and when they did, it was mostly at a level not requiring a great deal of research. Nevertheless, Brady didn't really seem to fit his preconception of a female detective. Where was the bullish loudmouth he had written about in the past? He had given the detective in Howl a continual need to prove herself all of the time, to everyone. She had been one of his least favourite characters to write about and had been more than happy to describe her death in lurid detail.

Brady wasn't like that at all. She was softly spoken, with a deliberate and intelligent manner about her which took you off guard. She was tiny in comparison with her colleagues too. All of this probably made her an easy character to underestimate. That, he knew, would be a mistake.

She had scrutinised him though. That was probably why she offered to bring him home, to have a look at him for herself, make her mind up about him. When she took his DNA and fingerprints, she was as close to him as Fleur had been. In any other circumstances, he would have found the smell of her perfume alluring. Apart from the smiles she frequently gave him, she was all business. Although she never went farther than the front room, her eyes were everywhere.

He supposed that was her training. To be nosy and to investigate. She'd scanned the room, which didn't take long given that it was largely bare. Even in the hallway, she glanced upstairs and did her best to look into the kitchen without it looking like she was *looking into the kitchen*.

So why hadn't he told her about the book? He had nothing to hide after all. Because he was afraid? Yes, but of what? Of failure, of losing the only thing he had ever been any good at – making up stories to scare people. He was frightened to death of that. That was what gave him nightmares, not some freaky clown breaking into the house in the middle of the night to help him rediscover his gift.

Until now.

Was it the same clown that tore Jim Crawley's body apart and covered his caravan in blood? It seemed ridiculous to think that it could be the same clown, yet it had to be. It had to be. So why hadn't Ben been butchered like Crawley? What made him different? He was using the outline the clown had given him but that was all. Other than that, there was no connection.

That same manuscript described the murder of a sick paedophile clown called Bingo. But that was inspired by the news, that was all. And the mutilation of the policeman, well that was just fantasy. He was sure he would have remembered seeing something like that on the television.

When was the last time he actually watched it?

He sat up and drank some of the lemon drink. The heat burned his throat but it wasn't anywhere near as harsh as it had been in the last few days. He didn't recall seeing the news since that obnoxious idiot DC Kelly visited. He picked up the remote and thought about putting the television on as a distraction, then thought better of it. He'd seen enough of human brutality to last him for today.

No, he convinced himself, it couldn't be the same person. The word 'Boo!' was his creation, and if somebody chose to use it as their own then so be it. That didn't necessarily make them a bad person; it didn't make them a killer.

He slumped back and opened his paperback. Nobody else was coming in the house today, with or without his permission, he made sure of that with Stan's help. But he needed a distraction to stop himself worrying about it. The barbarity of the act, the violence and the blood had knocked him off his feet. Literally. He had seen it and would probably keep on seeing it for years to come, but his brain kept trying to tell him it wasn't real, it was just a scene from one of his books. And yet no book he had ever written or read could even come close to what was in that caravan.

Maybe this evening he might go down to the office and write something. He smoothed Stan again, his teeth chattering with pleasure. If he couldn't get some inspiration from what had happened today, he had no business being a writer.

At just after seven, Ben finished the book and dropped it beside the bed. Stan stretched his long limbs and opened an eye to see what Ben was doing.

"Need a wee?" he asked the dog who pointed his ears upward and licked his lips.

"Yep, me too."

Ben rolled off the bed and padded to the bathroom. Stan followed behind and stood in the doorway to the en-suite.

He glanced in the mirror as he passed and rubbed his chin. "I need a shave," he said.

Even if the circumstances had been different, there was no way a woman like Brady would look twice at him. He looked like a tramp who had been on the streets for the last ten years, not a successful writer.

He finished in the bathroom and patted Stan on the head. "*Was* a successful writer, Stan. Was."

He reached the top of the stairs and peered into the gloom on the ground floor. He felt like a child who was afraid of the dark, but he couldn't bring himself to take the first step. He flicked the switch and the hallway was immediately illuminated.

"All the doors were locked, all the windows locked and neither you nor Stan heard a sound, so man up and get down there." He felt Stan's warmth on his thigh as the dog leaned on him.

He stopped breathing for a few seconds and listened. There were no alien sounds, just the chatter of Stan's teeth and the wind whistling across the fields outside. He started walking down the stairs. Maybe he needed to start thinking about protecting himself? He reached the hallway and flicked the switch to light up the lounge and the kitchen. Was it possible to obtain a shotgun? He had no idea what the process was or what the costs were, but it was something worth looking into.

He walked into the lounge and checked the windows again. He felt foolish but he knew he wouldn't be able to concentrate on writing if he thought there was a chance the house was unsecure.

Stan followed Ben into the kitchen. As soon as he had let the dog go out, he closed the door and locked it immediately. Stan would let him know when he was ready to come back in.

With the light on, he was blind to the fields outside. If

someone was out there watching him, he wouldn't have a clue. But the alternative was turning the lights off and that was definitely not an option.

He pulled a pepperoni pizza out of the freezer and pushed it into the oven. He didn't especially want to eat it or anything else, but his stomach felt empty and was starting to aggressively complain about the lack of food in it.

Stan had only been outside for half of his usual time but his whines at the back door were difficult to ignore, so Ben let him in. When the pizza was ready he took it into the study and sat down at his desk. The room wasn't really large enough to accommodate Stan too, but he wouldn't be left out and wedged himself in the corner. He looked uncomfortable as he hunkered down and closed his eyes.

Ben stared at the manuscript left by the clown for a long time before he could stand to pick it up. The pages seemed heavier than before. It was as if there was extra weight to the words, like they were written in blood instead of ink.

He rolled them up and dropped them into the waste basket. They weren't the words of killer, just a fan. A fan with some pretty good ideas but just a fan. Seeing what had happened to Jim had turned him upside down and shaken his guts around, but it was totally separate from what was happening here. If he had mentioned it to Brady, she probably would have laughed at him. He almost laughed himself, at his stupidity. Someone who did what they did to Jim wouldn't break into someone else's house on two occasions, just to bring them a half-written story? More likely they would have slaughtered him as he slept.

He stared at the manuscript and smiled. The writing was rudimentary at best, but filled with a creativity that sparked his own back into life. For that he was thankful, but the door was closed and locked now and he didn't need their help any more. He had never had a stalker but knew plenty of others did. If things got worse or changed direction, he would call the police and report it. He looked at the business card DS Brady gave him. Maybe she might pay another visit?

He smiled again and opened the word processor software on his computer. And if she did come back, he would have a shave and tidy himself up a bit. He tried his best to keep his eyes away from the tired reflection looking back at him from the small window to the side of his head.

For the first time in a very long time, he felt excited as he typed the title of his new book at the top of the page. He read it aloud: "Boo!"

This was going to put him back on the map.

At just after one in the morning, Ben saved the file and powered down. Not in a very long time had his creative juices flowed quite so freely. The tips of his fingers stung with the power and speed at which he typed. It was a wonderful feeling.

He probably could have gone on all night. In the past, he put in a lot of all-night sessions. But his body and head throbbed with the remnants of the flu. Without moving for the last four hours, his throat was on fire, not to mention the pain in his bladder. His body was telling him enough was enough. For now.

He arched his back and groaned as the muscles sighed with relief.

"Wee?" he asked Stan, who had only moved once during the same amount of time.

The dog sneezed and jumped to his feet in an untidy whirl of legs.

"Come on, then it's time for bed."

Stan followed him to the back door and shot out into the unfathomable darkness.

Ben had been writing long enough and was competent enough to know that what he had just typed was about as good a first draft as he was capable of. God, it felt good. He hadn't had to think very hard to bring the images of Crawley's blood-spattered caravan back to life, but surprisingly it hadn't made him feel sick. Instead it released a stream of creativity and energy which had overridden everything else. When he was flowing like that, all other concerns drifted away.

With a few tweaks and some sharp dialogue, he managed to put Sparkles back into his old life, back into his old diabolical ways. It felt right to do it. It was almost as if what he had seen this morning had been created just for him, just to inspire him to write again. He almost felt bad for taking inspiration from Crawley's death, but fact and fiction were always comfortable bedfellows for a writer.

He called the dog who burst inside like his arse was on fire. His coat was wet from a steady fall of rain. Ben dried him on an old towel hanging by the back door. Stan licked his face and chattered his teeth to show his appreciation. They both walked into the hall together but after Ben touched the light switch, he went back to the kitchen and pulled the carving knife from the wooden block. The adrenalin shot from writing had taken care of some of the anxiety caused by Crawley's murder this morning, but there was no harm in taking some protection to bed.

Stan stretched out beside him on the duvet, making contented grunts as he fell asleep. Ben knew that tonight he would also fall asleep quickly. When he wasn't writing, his mind was restless and agitated because it wasn't being exercised. It was the opposite sensation when he was writing: calm, relaxed and satisfied. He rolled over and put his hand on the cold steel of the knife's handle on the bedside table. Within a few seconds he was asleep.

*

It was a slow rise to the surface but once he got there, he didn't understand why he was awake. The room was completely dark so he knew it wasn't his body-clock telling him it was time to wake up. He rubbed his face, felt the bristles scrape across his skin. He was aware that Stan had shifted and was looking up at him.

He checked his phone, nudging the knife. Both fell to the floor with a dull thud but the phone lit up and told him it was nearly three-thirty. Way too early to wake up. He rolled back over, touched Stan's head and closed his eyes.

Thump, thump.

His eyes flicked open and his senses clicked into gear. What was that? He waited and listened, holding his breath, trying not to move.

Thump, thump, thump.

Was it in the room? Was *it* in the room?

No, it was too far away, downstairs somewhere. He took his hand off the dog. Stan was rigid, and in the gloom he could see he was staring at the door. He put his hand out to grab the knife but felt nothing except for the cover of his paperback. Where was it? A beacon of panic sparked up in the back of his head. If he let it burn for too long, it would flash through his brain and tie him to the bed in a useless heap.

The knife, he had to have the knife.

It was on the floor. He had knocked it off the table a few seconds ago. Stan made a long whine which turned into a growl at the end. The bed shook as the dog trembled.

Thump.

That was it. There was definitely someone in the house. How the hell had they got in? The windows were locked as were the doors.

The back door. Had he locked it again after Stan came in? He couldn't remember *not* doing it. But he couldn't remember doing it either. He reached down and grabbed the knife. There were some options. He could play dead and pretend to be asleep. That had worked in the past. Or he could grow a pair, go downstairs and… and what? Stab the intruder? He hadn't had a fight in thirty years, so if anyone was going to end up on the losing side it was him.

Thump, thump.

Stan growled and stood up on the bed. They were on the stairs. Whatever he was going to do, he had to do it now.

He rolled off the bed and patted his leg. The dog jumped

down and Ben winced. Stan wasn't light on his feet and the noise was deafening. They moved quickly across the carpet and into the en-suite. He locked the door behind them and pushed his back against the door. His heart was bouncing around in his chest at a thousand miles an hour. The sound echoed with a creepy thud.

Thump, thump, thump, thump.

They weren't on the stairs now, they were at the top. Waiting. Waiting. What were they waiting for?

And then there was the sound of the door scraping across the fibres of the carpet. Opening the door and coming into the bedroom. He clutched the knife in both of his hands and looked down at the dog. Please don't make a sound, he thought.

He could hear footsteps now. Soft and deliberate across the carpet as if tip-toeing, trying not to be heard.

"I am being quiet!" a whispered voice hissed.

Who were they talking to? Was there more than one of them? It didn't sound like there were two sets of feet on the carpet.

The voice hissed again. "He isn't here."

There were definitely two of them. Either that or someone was talking to himself. Ben's phone was on the floor beside the bed. Why hadn't he picked it up as well as the knife? He could be in here calling the police. Should he shout something? Something threatening?

He opened his mouth but Stan beat him to it and growled. If Ben didn't know better, he might have thought Stan was a ferocious beast. He had never heard anything like it from the dog before. Ben winced. There was no hiding where he was now.

Silence followed. It was the sort of silence that was truly deafening. Each beat of his heart seemed to reverberate up through his flesh and make an almighty boom. But there was nothing from the other side of the door.

He knows I'm in here and I know he's out there, thought Ben. He dropped his hand and turned the lock. Enough was enough, he would rush out screaming and shouting and start swinging. He looked down at Stan and the dog curled his lips back in a silent snarl. He swallowed twice. Now he had made the decision, all the moisture in his body had retreated somewhere. Just like his balls.

Time for us both to grow a pair, he thought, grabbing the handle. He turned it quickly and rushed into the bedroom roaring and swinging the knife wildly about.

After a few wild seconds he could see the room was empty, completely empty. He turned around again holding the knife out in front and jerking his head from side to side, but he was the only person in there.

The bedroom door was open though, and the darkness beyond was absolute. He could close the door, barricade himself in and call the police, that would be easy. That would be safe.

He looked down at Stan who was beside him. "You up for this?"

The dog whined and leaned on him. "No, neither am I but we're going anyway."

He ran forward. "I've got a knife!" he screamed. He

hoped his voice was more threatening than it
sounded to him.

As soon as he left the bedroom he felt vulnerable, and whatever false courage had been burning in his chest vaporised. He stopped at the top of the stairs, looked down and listened. Had they gone? The house was quiet apart from his and Stan's ragged breaths.

"Boo!" a whispered voice came from behind him.

He jumped and let out a grunt. As he whipped around, his stomach tried to force its way up his throat and into his mouth. He tried to swallow it back but there was no moisture. He heard the dog skidding across the carpet as he tried to run away.

Ben completed the turn and stepped back. He tried to raise the knife but his foot slipped off the top step and then he was falling backwards, down into the void, and looking into the face of his creation. Sparkles was watching him fall. On his face was the most god-awful sneer he had ever seen. It ran almost from ear to ear and it was sickening.

Then there was an intense pain on the back of his head and blackness.

15

It was light when Ben came to. He didn't open his eyes but the morning filtered through his eyelids in a grey haze. How long had he been out? Two, three, four hours? There was no way of telling but at this time of year it didn't get properly light until after seven. That would make it at least four hours. That was plenty of time for someone to cut off his face and chop him into little bits.

But he was alive. For some reason, he was alive.

He wriggled his arms and legs. There was soreness but nothing like the pain he'd experienced when he broke his arm three years ago. That was a pain he would never forget. The worst of it was at the back of his head. It felt like a bomb had gone off and blown part of his skull away. He gingerly lifted his head and touched his hair. There were no sticky clumps where blood had been spilled but it throbbed all the same.

He lowered his hand and stretched his arms out to the side. His fingers touched something and he knew immediately what it was. Paper. A ream of paper. Without looking, he knew there were words typed on it. Black words in neat little rows all strung together like the legs of dead spiders. That was why he was still alive. So he could write new stories using a real-life Sparkles as inspiration. A true collaboration.

He rolled over, away from the papers, and retched. "Stan!" he croaked. There wasn't the usual scrabbling of paws on the carpet in response. There was nothing. His heart sank. If anyone had hurt him, if anyone had laid a finger on the dog…

There was a whine and the sound of teeth chattering. Ben finally opened his eyes and where Sparkles had been when his eyes were last open was Stan's friendly face.

"Come on." He patted the carpet next to him and sat up. Stan whimpered and came slowly down the stairs. Stan had spent nearly all of his life as a working dog, as someone's asset at the racetrack. He didn't do the things that other dogs did, he didn't know how. He was ambivalent about most things and he certainly didn't know how to be brave or fierce. But as he lowered himself to the floor beside Ben and dug one of his elbows into a sore spot, Ben realised Stan was his best friend. He loved the dog more than any person alive and the dog was probably the only living thing that loved him. If he spent much time thinking about it, he might cry again. It was pretty sad.

*

Ben watched from the spare room as the police car come down the track toward the house. He held a damp tea-towel to the back of his head. The room had once served as Rachel's gym, but she took the equipment when she left and now it was an empty box. There were three others just like it. The house had felt cold and lonely for a long time but never more so than right at that very moment. He knew he should have moved a while ago but now the need was urgent.

So eager had he been to get back on top, to write another bestseller, that he had lost his way completely. Clutching at straws, someone else's straws, pretending that it was his own writing and even going so far as to risk his own life by talking himself into some irrational theory. He was a ridiculous man.

He was embarrassed by his own actions, by the way he had treated Rachel. And for god's sake, he had slept with a girl young enough to be his daughter, who had taken the piss out of him and posted his arse all over the internet. He was an embarrassing idiot, too caught up in his own importance to do the right thing. The right thing was to have phoned the police days ago. The right thing would be to crawl into the deepest hole and stay there until his bones crumbled into the earth.

He hadn't asked for Brady by name when he made the report to the operator. He simply reported a burglary. He knew once he started to tell the officers what had happened then she would be notified, but was too ashamed to tell her what he should have said yesterday.

He let the two officers in and told them what had happened. One of them, the younger one, was on his radio immediately.

"We're just calling through for some assistance. For a specialist to come and speak to you."

Ben nodded. "Detective Sergeant Brady?" he asked.

The officer looked shocked. "You know DS Brady, Mr Night?"

Ben walked toward the kitchen. "We met yesterday. I'll put the kettle on." There it was, he would have to tell her everything now. All of it. It wasn't going to be his proudest moment.

*

Within twenty minutes, Brady was standing in his kitchen with two other detectives.

"Have you called for a paramedic?" she asked one of the uniformed officers. His face reddened in reply.

"I don't need one." Ben lowered the towel and looked at the officer. "I'm okay."

Brady pushed the point. "We'll get someone here to give you the once-over. You were unconscious for a while, Mr Night."

Ben just nodded. He didn't have the energy to argue.

"The officers have already told me what you said to them but I'd like you to repeat it to me, please." Brady sat across the table from him while the other two detectives wandered off. She opened her book and took a pen from the inside her jacket.

Ben took a deep breath and recounted the events of last night. He was embarrassed about hiding in the toilet but she showed no discernible response to his narrative. She asked him to describe the clown's face several times, going over minor details again.

Was she trying to trip him up?

Finally she stood up and smiled. "We'll keep looking around and if you remember anything else, give me a shout. I'll be here for a while yet." Her smile made him want to smile back but he couldn't.

He grimaced as she turned away. "There is one other thing," he said quietly.

She turned around. "Yes?"

"Sparkles has been here before." He paused and then added, "Twice before."

"Sparkles?" Brady asked.

"Sparkles, Bingo, whatever you want to call him. It's all the same. Newman based his creation on my creation. They have the same face."

For a split-second, her facade slipped and Ben saw something akin to shock pass over her face. Then the control was back again. She sat down and opened her book.

"I think we need to have another chat then."

Ben told her about the first night Sparkles came to his room. How he had been ill and assumed the clown standing in the doorway was a dream or a hallucination, so he waved at it. In the morning he had found a few pages of manuscript which he assumed he had written while in the grips of a fever. He had seen the story about the paedophile clown's murder and thought that was where his inspiration came from.

On the second occasion, Sparkles had stood in his room

and written 'Boo!' in the frosted mirror. It all sounded so ridiculous, so utterly stupid that he could feel his face growing redder by the second. He had allowed a clown to come into his house and leave manuscripts on his desk and now he was telling a rational, logical detective why he hadn't reported it. He could barely stand to hear his own voice.

"But the second one wasn't connected to a real event, not like the first one. It was about a copper being killed. I don't…"

Brady interrupted for the first time. "Where are they?"

Ben pointed at the office. "In there, in the bin. Shall I fetch them?"

She shook her head. "Not yet. Can you remember how the police officer was killed?"

He nodded. "The clown tied him to a chair in front of a mirror and made the cop… policeman watch his own disfigurement and death. It was extreme, far more extreme than anything I would ever…"

"When was the last time you saw the news, Mr Night?"

He shrugged. "Couple of days ago, I suppose. Why?" The question seemed irrelevant to him.

"Because that is exactly how my colleague, DC Kelly, was found murdered. In front of a mirror. You met him, didn't you? He came here to ask you some questions about Sparkles."

Ben felt sick.

"And I bet if we look at that pile of papers in the hallway, that story will be about a circus worker murdered in his caravan."

He looked down at the table. Why was this all happening to him?

"I don't understand why you wouldn't report this to us. I don't get it."

Ben clenched his teeth together and looked up. "I'm lost." It wasn't the right moment to say it but it was a relief. "I'm utterly, totally and royally lost. I couldn't tell you which way was up at the moment and making the right decision has never been in my skill set."

He paused and enjoyed the slightly bewildered look in her usually cold eyes.

"I don't know if you've ever read my books, but I used to be able to write half-decent stories. I wrote Clownz when I was twenty. That's twenty-seven years ago. I can't believe it sometimes. It doesn't seem so long ago but it is, it's a very, very long time ago and I've been chasing it ever since. People liked my stories so I wrote some more but nothing has ever come close to Clownz. Nothing."

He paused, searching for the right words. "To be honest, it's the only thing I've ever known how to do properly. I'm shit at life but good at making up stories. Sounds pretty messed up, doesn't it?"

He didn't wait for an answer, he didn't need or want one, just looked down at the table again. "So imagine losing that part of you. Imagine losing half of your mind, half of your sense. How would you be then? You'd be a disaster zone, that's what. And that's what you're looking at here. I kept those manuscripts because I thought I could use them, I could write again. Sparkles's words would inspire me to write about him again. To bring him back to life. To make him real in here." Ben tapped the side of his head. These were things he should be talking about to a doctor, not a police officer.

"I can't write any more. I've no idea if I'll ever be able to again." He looked up and into her eyes again. "I'm sorry about your colleague and I'm sorry you've just had to listen to all that self-pity rubbish."

Brady dropped her pen. "Mr Night, I read Clownz last night and it scared the hell out of me. I've downloaded all of your books and I'm going to read them all. There's more stories in you yet. I'm sure of that."

Ben couldn't help himself and smiled. "You enjoyed it? Even after what you saw yesterday?"

"I did." Brady sighed and stood up again. "We just need to work out how we're going to catch Sparkles." She paused, picking up her book and pen. "And we need to work out why you're still alive."

She turned and walked toward the office. "Now, show me these manuscripts and we'll see if we can shake Sparkles's mask off."

He opened the office door for her. "This is where the magic happens," he said with a half-arsed smile and stepped aside.

"The bin's over there beside the desk." He pointed but the room was so small she couldn't miss it.

She nodded and walked across the little room.

"It's empty," she said, picking it up to show him. "There's nothing in here."

Ben walked to her. "What? I put the whole lot in there yesterday." He scanned the desk, the bookcase and even knelt to look under the computer table. There was nothing there. He rubbed his chin and remembered that he hadn't shaved again; how much like a tramp he must look.

"I don't get it." And then again to emphasise his point, "I don't understand."

"You're sure you dropped them in here?" Brady asked.

"Absolutely."

"Well they're not here now, so that means they are in the house somewhere or he took them with him for some reason. Anywhere else they could be?"

"No," he answered and turned out of the room. "But if he took them, why leave another manuscript for me? It doesn't make sense."

She walked past him and he followed. Stan followed close behind. All the strange people in the house was making him more anxious than normal.

Brady knelt by the bundle of papers in the hallway. "Have the papers been photographed?" she called to nobody in particular.

"Done!" someone shouted from upstairs.

He watched Brady take a pair of blue latex gloves from her pocket and put them on. He hadn't touched them, not even to look under the top sheet, but he could see that they hadn't been dropped there. The papers had been placed neatly down about two inches away from where his head was just a few hours ago. It made him feel sick to think how vulnerable he had been.

Brady lifted the top blank sheet with her fingertips, then the next one down, and carried on until she had gone through ten pages or more.

"They're all the same," she whispered but it was loud enough for Ben to hear.

He crouched down beside her. "Boo!" he said. It was typed on every page that she had turned and he had no doubt it would be the same all the way down. A cold chill ran along his spine, making him shiver.

"He wrote that on the mirror. In the vapour from his breath," he muttered.

"And in blood at all the scenes." She stood up. "It's what your creation says, isn't it? It's what Sparkles says to his victims just before he mutilates them."

Ben looked up at her and nodded. "Every time." He got to his feet and felt the hallway tilt slightly to the left. It took a moment to level off again.

"Perhaps you'd better sit down again. The paramedic should be here in a minute or two."

She took his arm and led him into the lounge. He flopped onto the sofa, Stan at his feet.

"I know DC Kelly asked you if you remembered Harvey Newman and you said you didn't, but is there anyone else you recall meeting, who struck you as being... odd? Any fans, someone you've corresponded with maybe?"

Ben shook his head. "In the last two years, apart from my agent, you're the only person I've spoken to for more than thirty seconds." He paused. "Well, there was one person but..." He immediately regretted bringing this up. It wasn't relevant, except to show her what sort of a person he was. If she didn't know already.

"Go on." Brady opened her book again and sat in the armchair.

"It was a girl I met at a signing last week. But she wasn't strange, apart from the fact that she slept with me. I suppose that makes her…"

"And what was her name?" Brady interrupted.

"Fleur something or other." This was deeply embarrassing. Brady's opinion of him must have been low but this would make it sink even further. "I don't recall her last name but you can find it easily enough."

"Yes?"

Ben grimaced and exhaled through his teeth with a hiss. "She's got some pictures of me on her Facebook page. They're not the best."

"Drunk or something?"

He looked for a sign that she was teasing him but her expression gave nothing away.

"Or something." There was no use in being delicate about it. Brady would see the photographs anyway. "If you type in my name and put 'naked' next to it, you'll see what I mean. But she tricked me, she left…" There was no use in trying to explain it, he would just dig himself deeper into the hole.

"Oh. Right."

Was that the trace of a smirk on her mouth? It was gone so quickly that he couldn't be sure.

"But as I said, she wasn't the sort of person to do

something like… like what was done to Jim Crawley or DC Kelly." He shrugged. "But then again, as you can see, I'm no judge of character."

Brady finished writing and clipped her pen to the top of her book. "Have you got anywhere else you can stay for a while?"

Ben shook his head. "No, but I'm not leaving anyway." It was all well and good saying that now, when the house was full of people and it was still daylight. He was trying to regain some semblance of credibility in front of Brady. Would he feel the same way at midnight?

Brady stood up and looked out of the window. "Looks like the paramedic's turned up."

What Ben needed was a bucket of painkillers and some sleep.

She looked at him again. "If you're going to stay, you might want to make sure the back door is locked as well as the windows. I'll see what I can do to add to your security."

She walked away leaving that cryptic comment hanging in the air, and opened the door for the paramedic.

16

Jane made it all the way back to the station before she realised she was actually driving a car. Ninety per cent of her brain was engaged in the investigation; going over and over possibilities and enquiries, trying to keep tabs on everything that was going on. The other ten per cent was trying to keep her alive; completing the tasks which took less thought, like telling her when to brake and change gear. She had engaged autopilot. It was a dangerous line to tread but entirely necessary. If she wanted to stay focused on her job, it was the only way.

She was pleased that Night had chosen to stay in his house, although she doubted his courage would be quite so muscular later tonight when it was dark. She was happy with his decision because he was the only link they had to 'Sparkles'. Keeping that link alive was what mattered. He was the key to all this, she just had to work out why and how. If she could do that, she would catch the clown.

Surveillance on Night and his house wouldn't be difficult

to obtain, given the circumstances. No doubt about it, someone would probably still want Night arresting; someone high up and detached from the investigation. Her resolve that he was not responsible had not wavered in the slightest, in fact after last night it was stronger than ever. Night's decision-making capabilities were offline, if they had ever been online in the first place, but he wasn't a killer.

Judging by his writing he had a very vivid, some might say sick, imagination but he wasn't who they were after. That didn't mean she hadn't told the officers to have a good look around while they were there. Police officers didn't need much encouragement to go snooping about in people's drawers and wardrobes. When those cupboards belonged to a minor celebrity, the urge was doubly strong. They just had to be subtle about it.

Night was a strange one. On the surface, and to people on the outside, he had everything a person could ask for. A great career he loved, a huge house, clearly plenty of money and he was handsome, in a dishevelled sort of way. But if you scratched away the polish, you found a confused and lonely individual. In trying to reach out for someone or something to help him regain his magic touch, he had plunged deeper into the hole he was already inhabiting.

Nevertheless, he had that 'chaotic artist' thing going on which she found oddly attractive. She smiled to herself. She had teased him about the photograph of his arse. She saw it the day before when she was conducting research on him. The picture was everywhere, linked to his name hundreds of times. There were even articles discussing the shape of it.

Her stomach gurgled in protest at lack of food. She turned off the main road away from the station toward the city centre. There was a shop which sold the best BLTs in the world. A BLT, a Snickers bar and a can of Tango were what she needed. She would worry about her gym schedule when this was all over but for now that's what she wanted.

Her phone rang just as she pulled up outside the deli. The display said DI White, his name flashing with each vibrating ring. She stared at it until it was silent and then opened her door. Her mouth started watering at the smell of freshly baked bread and fried bacon. She could almost taste it. Missing meals was usual but she couldn't remember when she had last eaten some real food.

The phone rang before she had a chance to close the door. White again. She looked at the shop then climbed back into the car.

"Boss?"

"Where are you, Jane?" He sounded excited.

"I was just about to grab something to eat." She looked at the deli again. The smell of bread and bacon had already gone.

"You might want to come back in."

"What have you got?" She could feel her taste buds closing up.

"Crawley's DNA. You need to see this. It's good."

"I'll be back in two minutes." She started the car and drove back toward the station. As good as White thought Crawley's DNA was, she knew it wouldn't compare to a freshly made BLT. Nowhere near.

*

She walked straight into White's office. He was sitting at his desk and didn't acknowledge her presence. By the look of him, he wouldn't notice if King Kong was sitting on his desk taking a crap.

"Boss?"

He looked up and rubbed his face. The dark circles under his eyes had grown over the last twenty-four hours and his skin had a yellowy, waxy tint to it. He sat in his chair awkwardly, putting all his weight on one cheek.

"You okay?" she asked.

"Yeah, yeah, I'm fine, just my back giving me some grief again. Pass me that box would you, please?"

He didn't look fine at all and she felt bad for him. She passed him the box of paracetamol tablets. He dry-swallowed four in one go and tapped one of his screens. "Have a look at this."

Jane walked around the desk and crouched down beside him. She scanned over the screens quickly to get an idea of what she was supposed to be looking at. On one side was Jim Crawley's DNA profile, gathered from his destroyed body, and on the other side was a list of hits on that DNA. Twelve hits, twelve unsolved rapes from around the country.

"Shit," she whispered.

"Indeed," White replied. "Some might say our clown is doing a public service taking people like this out of circulation. A dead paedophile and a dead rapist is hardly a great loss to society. Where does that leave Stu Kelly, I wonder?"

Jane ignored the comment. "Any local ones?" She grabbed the mouse and moved it down the list.

"Not yet but two came in during the last five minutes. There's going to be more, I reckon."

She read the women's names silently. "How is this possible? Crawley must've been known to us."

White moved in his chair and Jane heard him emit a grunt. It sounded like pain.

"No trace of him. If he's ever been in trouble, it was a long time ago. Before we started using DNA."

She stood up. "Anyone else seen this yet?"

"Not yet. I'm going up to brief Hargreaves in a minute. I'm emailing it to you now. Can you get someone to start phoning the other forces? Get them to speak to the victims and see if we've got anything we can use?"

Jane was still thinking about how best to use Ben Night but she nodded.

"How was it this morning? Hargreaves will want to know." White got slowly to his feet. He squeezed his eyes shut as he did so.

She walked around the other side of the desk. "It looks legitimate. Unsecure back door, clown comes in and gives Night a scare, sending him down the stairs. I'll write it up and put it through HOLMES but that's the essence of it."

White nodded and took a clumsy step forward. "Anything else?"

Jane nodded. "Now here's where it gets interesting." She told him about the other visits from the clown and about the manuscripts. White let out a long sigh.

"If I can get the surveillance paperwork finished tonight, will you sign it?" she asked.

White winced. "Of course but you might have to bring it to me at home."

He hobbled around the desk and Brady made way for him to get through the door. "I'll text you my address," he added, then put his hand on her shoulder. "Everything they told me about you was true, Jane. You're incredible."

She smiled back, embarrassed at the compliment. "Thank you."

White shuffled down the corridor like an old man. However bad he looked sitting down, he looked ten times worse trying to walk. She walked across the empty office and sat at her desk. There was nobody to phone around the other police forces. As much as she detested it, she was the only one she trusted to complete the surveillance paperwork properly. It was going to be a long night again.

She opened White's spreadsheet and started working through it. Within half an hour, she was becoming frustrated with the lack of progress. In a time when information was supposed to flow freely between forces, she was met with restrictions, demands for authorisation and additional form-filling before she would be given access to the rape files.

"Thanks for being so helpful," she said and slammed the phone down. She would ask one of the team to complete the necessary forms and submit them in the morning. There was only one left on the list anyway. If that was another closed door, she could move onto the surveillance paperwork knowing she could do no more for the time being.

The final two rapes had taken place in one district but were several years apart. She dialled the number, bypassing the automated message to speak to an actual person in the control room. She introduced herself and explained what she wanted.

She was prepared for a knock-back but instead heard the operator tapping away on his keyboard.

"Ah yes, I remember these. If they'd been closer together, they would have made the national news."

"Oh?" Jane asked. She was conscious that she had already obtained more information than in all the other calls put together and didn't want to push too hard.

"Okay, so the first one is from 1999. I've not got the whole file here, you would normally have to request it but I can give you a précis?"

Jane couldn't believe her luck and opened her book. "Yes please."

"Victim was a Marie Clulow born March 74. Well-known street worker who is sadly no longer with us. MO states she was grabbed from behind and pushed into the bushes. Then raped."

She took the details but there was nothing remarkable about it.

"She said the suspect looked like a creepy clown."

Jane felt the moisture leave her mouth and an icy chill went down her back. It took her a moment to speak. "A clown?"

"That's right. The other one's the same, only about four years later."

The operator gave her the MO which Brady wrote verbatim in her book, but she barely heard him for the noise in her head. They already knew Crawley was a rapist but his MO was new. Had nobody thought to put all this together before? It had happened all over the country but surely someone would have seen the connection?

The image of the scene inside the caravan flashed through her mind. Crawley's mashed-up face with bits of plastic clown mask embedded deep in his flesh. Was that the mask he wore when he committed the atrocious crimes? Jane found she was clenching and then unclenching her fists, one after the other. It had been the most violent scene by far. Where the other two had been controlled and staged, this had been chaotic and savage.

A revenge killing? It was possible. It was also possible there were multiple suspects out there. One a victim of 'Bingo' and the other the victim of a serial rapist. So where did that leave Stu? It left him a murder victim and one without a sordid secret, nothing more.

This gave them a whole new set of enquiries. A nasty set with tentacles that stretched all over the country. She shivered and closed the window behind her. Outside, Derby was winding down for the day. The roads out of the centre were great curving tails of red light, as the drivers battled to get home. And out there somewhere was a lunatic carving people's faces up with his knife.

She sat back down. Crawley was worse than an animal and the world was better off without him, just like the world was better off without Harvey Newman. The thought of

Crawley doing what he did to those women while wearing that mask was utterly repulsive, and she could feel her face muscles twitching with disgust. But that didn't matter. What mattered was that she was going to catch the clown. That was her job, she wasn't a judge.

She brought up the forms for surveillance authority, wincing when she saw what was expected. She should probably contact White and tell him what she had found out, but judging by the state of him, he would be at home now. She would tell him later when she took the paperwork to his house.

It still niggled her that getting the information from the other forces had been so difficult. They were all on the same team, weren't they? Some of it was old information so she could understand…

Her thoughts changed direction with an almost audible click. None of Crawley's victims lived on her patch, at least none they knew of. Which seemed strange given that they knew his circus had visited Derbyshire on at least five occasions. But what if there were victims, just that they hadn't got to the stage where DNA had been taken, or they were too old?

Her thoughts went back to the rape allegation she and Stu had got into trouble over. She had been kept out of the interview room while Stu talked to her. He sent her off on some ridiculous goose-chase and spoke to the girl alone. It was never recorded as a crime, and Stu convinced her it hadn't happened. But what had she said to him? There were probably countless others treated the same way over the years. Thank god policies had changed. Still, there was something about it, about the proximity to the current investigation and the timeliness of it that made her feel uneasy. Where to start though? Where on earth to start?

She went into the crime reporting program and searched through the database using MO keywords, terms including 'mask' and 'clown'. The software was badly out of date but it was capable of completing simple searches like this without a problem.

It threw up a few reports but nothing to match exactly what she was looking for. She drummed her fingers on the desk, staring at the screen. It was something she would have to ask the analysts to do in the morning but they wouldn't thank her for it.

She closed down the program, and the window containing Stu's workload popped up. She had gone through his last few tasks this morning to make sure there was nothing they were missing. Then the call had come through about Night's house so it had been left.

It contained a record of all of his tasks on this enquiry and, as his last supervisor, she had access to his previous investigation history. That included every incident, every crime he had attended. It also contained every report he ever wrote. It was, in essence, his life as a police officer.

She moved the pointer to the scroll bar and stopped. She knew what she was looking for, she knew exactly where it would be, but it didn't feel right to go through his notes like this. It was as if she was judging him, somehow. Scrutinising how he had worked.

She clicked the button and scrolled the screen. To hell with it. If there was anything on that specific report then it might be crucial. It might be another link to the killer. Finding him was more important that any scruples about examining a dead man's work.

She moved down to the date and clicked on the incident. When she was interviewed by Professional Standards, they asked her repeatedly what the girl had said and what Stu said in response. They wanted to know what happened in that room but she hadn't been there, she had been off on an enquiry. When Stu came out, he said the girl had made it up in a heroin-induced haze. She was as high as a kite, Stu had said, and the girl simply looked vacantly at the wall.

"What did she say, Stu?" Jane opened up his report and started reading.

'The informant is a Tanya Hayes (28/4/70) of 12b Gladstone Street. She reported to police that she had been raped on Shaftesbury Street Park at approximately 3am on Thursday 30th September 2004. Myself and DC Brady have spoken to Hayes and she does not now wish to report a crime. She stated to myself that she made the allegation up as a daydream due to her drug abuse. She is refusing to cooperate with a police investigation and shows no sign of injury. I do not believe this incident has occurred. Hayes has shown signs of drug use during our conversation and she does not appear lucid or in control of her thoughts. She has twice mentioned that there is a clown hiding in the bushes on Shaftesbury Park. Both DC Brady and myself saw no signs of clowns when we were there earlier. We will ensure Hayes is returned to her address but I request that

no crime is recorded in light of the information above. DC Kelly.'

Jane saw the word and it jarred her. She would have to double-check the dates on the circus calendar, but she knew the mention of a clown was no coincidence. In all her years, the only time she had seen the word 'clown' on a crime report was during the last week. The clown in the bushes at Shaftesbury Park was Jim Crawley.

She printed a copy of the report and searched for the name Tanya Hayes. Three came up but only one was a match. Tanya Hayes died from an overdose three years ago. There was a connection between what was happening now and what happened then. How was the connection formed though, and what did it mean? It would need a discussion with Hargreaves and White to see where they went with it, if anywhere. White would want to see it before Hargreaves got involved. She owed it to him to show him before the morning briefing.

She checked her watch. It was getting close to ten o'clock already. If she didn't get her arse in gear and the surveillance paperwork sorted, she wouldn't get to White until after midnight. She couldn't imagine he would be too happy about that. Especially in his current condition.

"Need any help?" She was so deep in thought that she hadn't heard two detectives come into the office.

She looked up and smiled. "No ta, get yourselves home please."

They both nodded. "See you in the morning."

She waved and carried on typing.

17

Jane put the car heater on full-blast. It was getting cold and soon she would have to start scraping the frost off the windscreen every morning. She hated doing that, it made her fingers scream.

White had sent her a text message over an hour ago with his address, asking how long she was going to be. She lied and told him ten minutes, but the form had been a bitch and even now she wasn't totally happy with it. As long as White was happy though, that was all that mattered; as long as the surveillance was granted.

It was half-past midnight now, so by the time she got home it would probably be after three. Three hours sleep and back in the office for seven. How long could she keep this up? How long would the adrenalin keep her body alert and alive? It wasn't as if she was twenty-one any more, she was forty-six and starting to feel it.

Fortunately, White only lived twenty minutes away from the station so as long as he didn't tell her to make alterations, this could be a quick visit. She knew he was unlikely to request too much because she knew more about it than him.

She pulled up outside and climbed out. It was like any other middle-class suburban street; all manicured lawns and clipped hedges. It suited her perception of White down the ground. She checked the house number on her phone and walked up the drive, past White's Audi. It was a typical 1930s detached property with bay windows on the ground floor and front bedrooms. It looked well cared for. Was he married? Did he have kids? She realised she didn't know much about him.

The only light on in the house, in the entire street, was what she supposed was the front bedroom. It was a perfectly natural place to be at this time of the night. She pressed the doorbell and heard the metallic ring inside. If he was married and had children, the noise would have woken the whole house. If that was the case then he should have told her to text him when she was outside. There, she knew one more thing about him now. He lived alone, just like her.

She didn't miss not having anyone to keep the light on for her. Not much anyway. The last guy who had kept the light on only did it so he could question her about where she had been until so late. That was the first and last time he asked her any questions. It was also the last time she saw him. Good riddance.

She wasn't tall enough to see through the half-moon shaped pane of glass at the top of the door, so she pressed the bell again. Maybe White had fallen asleep waiting for her. She didn't blame him for that.

"Come on," she whispered and stared at the door, willing it to open. The longer she waited, the longer it would be before she could climb into bed.

After two more minutes, there was still no answer. White had definitely fallen asleep but she wasn't prepared to leave it until the morning. Not now she had stayed so late to get it finished. She took her mobile out of her bag and found his number. She hoped he hadn't got so fed up with waiting that he'd turned his phone to silent.

It rang and rang then went to his answerphone message. She cancelled the call before the message finished. What was she going to do now? She dialled his number again and walked down the drive to look up into the window. There were no signs of life up there, just the dull orange glow of a small lamp.

She looked back at her car. She should just go home and brief him about Stu and Crawley in the morning. She cancelled the call before it reached the answerphone and walked toward her car. She should be asleep just like everyone else on the…

There were no other cars parked on the road except hers and another one a little farther down the street. It looked out of place in an area like this. It had the *blocky* design of her first ever car, like a car made in the Eighties, and the front bumper hung down slightly at one corner. A bad feeling nibbled at the base of her skull and she turned back toward White's house. Was that movement in the bedroom? She was sure a shadow had just passed across the ceiling.

She dialled his number again, walking back up the drive.

The nibble had turned into a bite. This time she left a message.

"Boss, it's Jane Brady, I'm outside your house now. Can you come down and let me in please?"

She kept her eyes on the bedroom and ended the call. There it was again, and this time there was no mistaking it. Someone was moving about up there. She rang the bell and then banged on the door. She started to think about finding Stu and felt sick. Almost immediately she gave herself a silent telling-off. There was no reason to think there was any connection with what had happened to Stu.

But if he was in there, why wasn't he answering? And that car, so badly out of place on a middle-class street like this. It was just the type of car the clown would go for. If she ran a check on it, she had a strong feeling it would come back as stolen. She didn't have time though, she needed to do something more decisive. She closed her eyes, wished she was at home in bed and asleep. But when she opened them again, she was still in the same place.

Jane looked around the side of the house. There was a six-foot high wooden gate blocking her view into the back garden. She doubted whether the street lights would be strong enough to illuminate much farther anyway. She didn't want to go round there, not one bit, but instinct told her she had to.

She walked to the gate and pushed it. Part of her hoped it wouldn't open and she would have no choice but to call it a day or phone for backup. But the gate creaked open. She stepped into the shadows beyond.

Her eyes adjusted quickly, it wasn't quite as dark as she first feared. Street lights from the avenues to the rear cast an weak glow into the garden. She activated the torch app on her phone too. It was far from ideal but better than nothing.

There was a large conservatory jutting out from the back of the house. She found the double doors and put her hand out to open it.

"Please, let it be locked," she whispered, pushing down on the handle. It opened easily and it was then she saw that the lock had been pushed through. Not just pushed through, obliterated. The door swung inward and scraped the destroyed lock against the laminate floor.

She reached into her harness and grabbed the radio. She had switched it off hours ago. The constant chatter did nothing for her concentration when she was trying to fill in the surveillance forms. She pressed the button to switch it back on.

"NA from DS Brady."

The answer came back immediately. "Go ahead."

"Can I have all available units to 55 Watson Avenue, please? I've got a break in progress."

"DS Brady, all local units are committed at the public order incident. I'll see if I can send officers from another division. Stand by."

Jane held the radio to her lips and considered her options. Someone from another division meant they were at least ten minutes away, possibly more. She could go in alone, CS gas at the ready. It was stupid thing to do but there was something wrong here, very wrong, and she didn't want to risk White's safety or losing the suspect.

"DS Brady, I've got a dog unit en route to the public order. He's diverting to you. He's fifteen minutes away. Can you contain the break?"

Of course she couldn't contain it. "I'll do my best."

She withdrew her gas, flipped the lid and stepped inside.

The conservatory led directly into the kitchen-diner. She stepped slowly through both rooms until she reached the hallway. The stairs led upwards on her right and another room was off to her left. An orange glow filtered through the window on the front door, shining onto the wooden floor. She walked toward the inner door and paused to listen. It was silent; everywhere was silent.

Jane pushed the front room door gently with her foot. It opened without a sound and she took a step inside. The room was lit by the same street light coming through the front door. There was a television in the corner, two sofas and a bookcase. Nothing more.

She turned out and stood at the foot of the stairs. Her heart was booming in her ears, made louder by the silence of the house. It was deathly. She had been as quiet as she could so it was still possible that whoever was in the house was unaware of her being inside. It was better that way. She had the element of surprise, she hoped.

The stairs were covered in carpet. She tested the bottom step. It creaked but it was soft, at least beside the crash of her heart. Jane put her bag down at the foot of the stairs and slipped her phone into her pocket. She took the rest of the stairs as quickly and quietly as she could, holding her little gas can out in front of her like a gun. The mellow light from the lamp in the front bedroom showed her the way.

She reached the landing and got her bearings. All the doors were closed except for the front bedroom but from where she was standing, she couldn't see inside. Each breath seemed to echo off the walls, giving notice of her presence.

Slowly, she worked her way toward the bedroom. Two metres away, she stopped and cocked her head. There was a low-pitched hum coming from the bedroom. A low-pitched tune. She recognised it in an instant. Carnival music, the type they play at a circus when the clowns come rolling into the arena. Someone was humming it. Her stomach cartwheeled as the picture of Stu Kelly's butchered face flashed across her mind.

There was no time to think about that, she had to act. She took the last few steps quickly, not caring if she alerted the killer to her presence. She held the gas out in front and ran into the room.

She gasped when she saw what was happening in the mirror. White's dead eyes – she hoped he was dead – stared at her in reflection. A clown stood behind him like a barber, slowly cutting around White's mouth. She could hear the knife slicing through his flesh and his humming was louder now, creepier and out of tune.

The clown looked away from his reflection and for a split–second, his eyes met hers. His own mutilated face, so pale, like death itself, was framed in her mind forever.

He smiled a hideous, malformed grin and whispered, "Boo!"

Jane thought of nothing other than bringing him to the floor and choking the life out of him. She rushed forward. She could hear high-pitched laughter as the edges of her vision closed in. It wasn't in the instruction manual but as she ran forward, she sprayed gas in front of her like a shield. It was only as she hit that shield that she realised she had gassed herself as well as the clown.

"Police officer, drop the knife!" she screamed.

The clown tried to jump to the side to avoid the spray, but had still been hit by a good dose. It was impossible to avoid it. He was standing with his back against a bank of built-in wardrobes and there was blood everywhere. It was on the carpet, on the clown, dripping from his knife in thick globules.

She crashed into him with her eyes stinging, her vision almost gone entirely. She hoped he was in a similar condition. She heard him grunt as she lashed out with her fist. She had no idea where she had caught him but it felt hideous, almost slimy.

She knew the knife was her main threat. He was holding it in his right hand. She turned away from that side and brought her left knee upwards with a sharp motion. It was aimed at his balls but she knew from the impact that it caught his inner thigh only.

She blinked rapidly but the gas was biting into her eyes, which watered with a thousand tears. Almost blind, she made a grab for the wrist holding the knife and smashed it into the wardrobe three times before he reacted.

He was taller than her but not well-built or particularly

strong. Nevertheless he managed to bring his free elbow up and smash it under her chin. She heard her teeth crack together as her head jarred backwards. Jane knew if she let go, she was done for. The gas was empty and by the time she racked her baton he would be on her, on her with the knife sticking in her throat. All that was left was her strength and her fight.

"Drop the knife!" she hissed at him and swung her other knee into his thigh.

Somebody screamed then and it wasn't her. It hadn't come from the clown either. That meant it came from White. He was still alive. The shock made her momentarily lose her strength. The clown seized his chance and shoved her backwards.

She staggered away from him, looking at White's reflection in the mirror. His eyes were bulging and as he opened what was left of his mouth, blood gushed out and rolled down his chin.

Jane felt a scream rise in her throat but there was no air left in her body to push it out. She watched White's head slump forward. It only took a second but it felt like longer. It was enough time for the clown to deliver a powerful punch to the side of her face. The blow knocked her off her feet and she sat, dazed on the blood-soaked carpet.

She looked up at the clown through stinging, foggy eyes. He was the stuff of nightmares. His face was a warped patchwork of skin and in there somewhere was a part of Stu Kelly and Jim Crawley.

Anger pushed away the shock. She tried to get back on

her feet. Her legs didn't feel like her own and they wouldn't stand under her. She groaned, crawled across the carpet.

"You're under arrest for murder, you..." Then his fist came down on her face again and a massive white light lit up her vision like a nuclear bomb. She collapsed face-first onto the carpet.

*

Jane screamed. She screamed like she had never screamed before, stinging her throat like acid on its way out. But she could feel his knife cutting through her skin. Deeper and deeper through the strata of her flesh, the sharp and dirty blade sank. He was trying to cut her eye out, trying to tease it from the socket so he could use it as his own. His face was beside hers. It was wan and ghostly; a patchwork of Newman, Kelly, Crawley and White all mashed together in a slimy, greasy leather. Dripping. Dripping slowly onto the carpet where it swirled into the fabric and made a vile soup.

Her stomach heaved and she screamed out a torrent of yellow liquid onto that same carpet. She was alive. She was alive and wasn't being cut into pieces. Her eyes felt like someone had attempted to remove them, though. As she tried to open her one good eye, a stab of pain sliced through her skull and flew out in a great steaming hiss from between her swollen lips.

Why am I not dead? she thought, looking at the back of White's head. Why am I not just like him? A blue strobe flashed across the mirror she could not stand to look into. Was she in the circus?

"Steady," a voice said from beside her. Panic flew

through her body like an angry hornet. She flailed her arms about and screamed again.

"It's okay, it's okay."

A hand gently touched her shoulder and she turned her head. A female police officer in a bright yellow jacket smiled down at her.

"Paramedics are on the way. Just lie still."

She rolled over. "It's not my blood," she said. When she tried to open her other eye again, she knew it was swollen shut. "The clown, where's the clown?" She knew she sounded almost hysterical. It wasn't through fear though, it was because she didn't want him to get away.

"Gone by the time I got here. Helicopter's up and another dog handler's on the way but we've lost him."

"Shit," Jane hissed, shuffling onto her bum. She found the courage to look at White's reflection. The clown had clearly finished the job he was part-way through when she interrupted him, but in a hurry. A lump of skin hung from White's cheek. She didn't need to ask whether he was alive, he couldn't be. It was better that way.

How long had he been tortured before she arrived? A wave of emotion swept over her. Tears fell from her cheeks.

"How long have you been here?" she asked.

"About ten minutes. Not long."

Jane leaned on the officer as she got to her feet. The room started spinning, first one way then the other. She had never been very good on rollercoasters. She closed her eye but it was no good, the world was moving around her and she couldn't stop it.

"How many units have we got looking for him?" Her lips felt enormous and her words sounded distorted but still intelligible.

"The helicopter, and two others, another dog unit on the way and me in –"

"The car! What about the car, is it still there?"

"What car?"

Jane took a step forward, and nearly fell. The officer held her arm. "I don't think you should be mo…"

"We need more. He couldn't have got very far." She felt groggy but her mind was slowly kicking into gear. She hadn't been out of it for that long. There was still a chance to get something out of this mess. There was still a chance to get the bastard. She couldn't even say what make of car it was. She hadn't looked closely enough. Maybe she should have, maybe she should have run a check on it but she wanted to get inside, she wanted to make sure White was… "CSI's on the way? What about the DCI?"

"I'm not sure, comms were…"

"Where's my radio? My bag?" She remembered leaving it at the bottom of the stairs but she needed it. She needed to start directing the search, calling for more troops. "It's at the bottom of the stairs," she said to herself and tried to walk, but her legs gave way and she fell to the floor.

"That's it. Do… not… move!" the officer shouted. A second later, Jane heard her galloping down the stairs.

"There's nothing here!" she shouted up. "There's no bag."

Jane groaned. He had access to a police radio now, he

could hear everything they were saying, could follow their search pattern. He also had her bag. She tapped her pocket, which was empty. He had her phone too.

She crawled onto the landing and slumped against a wall. Being in that room, in that hell, for another second was just too much. She lifted her hands to her face and tried to pick a strand of hair away from her eye but it was stuck, glued to her face by White's blood.

Jane slammed her fists into the carpet as hard as she could and sobbed.

18

"That was close, buddy-boy!"

Maldon drove quickly through the suburban streets, his eyes stinging and nose running. The police radio was on the seat next to him, along with the tall, bald policeman's face. The radio was buzzing with chatter about what he'd just done.

He could already feel the telltale *itch* that always came after. It was his smile growing, millimetre by glorious bloody millimetre. By the time he fixed the smile properly onto Sparkles, it would run from ear to ear. It couldn't get any wider. But all was not well.

He knew the police would eventually 'sting' the radio so his time was limited, but he listened to the confused mass of voices and changed his route accordingly. It wasn't difficult, he had ten minutes start on them.

It was a good job the woman officer kept her diary in her bag. In the back were all of her passwords, including one for the radio. She was pretty. Even though she had tried to knee him in the balls, she was really very attractive.

He took her phone as much out of curiosity as anything, but it gave him a thrill to reach into her pocket and take it. Her trousers were tightly stretched over her thigh as she lay in the bloody sponge of carpet. It made the rectangular outline of her phone stand clear through the fabric. As he reached into her pocket, he felt the warmth of her flesh seep through his gloves, making him shudder. It wasn't affection, she was unconscious, but it was the heat of another human being, a person who was not an evil life-sucker like these others. It was an electrifying sensation, one he had not felt for a very long time. It had made him jerk away and almost fall backwards.

Sparkles had urged him not to do it again, had threatened him, but it was too much and he removed a glove and slid his hand back inside her pocket. Her skin burned through the thin fabric and sizzled on his own. He had groaned at the pleasure of it. It was warmth, it was tenderness. It was alien.

Sparkles had heard the sirens in the distance. It was Sparkles whose voice screamed above the crash of his heart and told him to move.

"Go, go, go!" Sparkles had bellowed into his ear. The strength of his voice pushed Maldon away, skidding across the carpet and into the wall.

He gripped the steering wheel harder and tried to ignore the tingle of electricity that still wriggled through his fingers; his ungloved, unprotected fingers. But her touch had not widened his smile, as he thought it might. No, it had diminished it. Just by a touch, an almost undetectable amount, but it was there, just at the corners of his deformed and mutilated lips. A lessening. He wasn't angry about it, not as he had been when the others took his smile. No, this time he felt... sad. He felt very, very sad.

"Cry baby custard, cry baby custard," Sparkles sang as he drove. Maldon didn't react. He didn't know how to.

He drove to the car park near his house, intending to torch the car. Intent on finishing the job he had started. Instead he just sat there for a while and listened to the early morning silence. Occasionally a vehicle would drive past on the main road, but mostly there was just an eerie silence which he found hypnotising.

He was no stranger to this time of day. Indeed, he had spent a good deal of his life prowling the streets looking for houses, sheds and cars to break into. But for the first time, he heard the night. His mind was silenced, the anger was gone and its absence was frightening. It was his compass, his purpose, his reason. It was who he was. He had carried it around for so long that he didn't know what, or who, he was without it.

He touched his face and felt the cold, miserable skin of three dead men under his fingers. He would add the tall policeman's flesh to it now. It was the last piece of the picture and it would finally give him his smile back completely.

But then what? Where would he go?

He adjusted the mirror and took the tube of superglue

from the glovebox. He hadn't had time to do a neat job in the house, so he took his bloody knife and carved the skin into the shape he needed, making sure to keep the lips intact. His knife cut through dead flesh easily and sliced through the cheap plastic seat too. When he was happy, he covered it in glue and held it up to his face. His reflection was awful, truly hideous. There were bits and pieces of face sticking out all over the place, layer on layer of dead flesh, all piled up into a revolting, greasy mask. Watery discharge oozed from his nose and mingled with dried blood.

He pushed the last piece into place, just below his ears and he gasped. All at once he was transformed. Gone was the repellent facade and in its place was a young boy. A grinning, laughing lad with a carefree look in his eyes. A beautiful boy without a worry in the world.

He touched the mirror with a bloody finger. It was him. It was Maldon Williams before… before the clown took everything from him.

And then it was gone. He twisted the rear-view mirror around and around until it snapped and fell into his lap. Sparkles looked up at him with that maniac grin and laughed.

"You can take the boy out of the clown, but you can't take the clown out of the boy!"

He had done everything Sparkles asked. Everything he had been told would bring about his own real smile. And yet they were *all* dead and it hadn't worked. Sparkles had lied. The smile on his face wasn't his own and he felt no different. Why, why, why?

Maldon slammed the car into gear and raced out of the car park. He knew where he had to go. The only person who knew what clowns were really like.

19

The door to Jane's apartment swung open. She reached inside to press as many light switches as she could. The alarm chirruped and flashed a lurid green on the wall opposite. The house was secure so she stepped inside and closed the door behind her. As she tapped the security code into the key pad, she was glad she had committed it to memory and not written it in the back of her diary like all the other passwords.

She took a deep breath and walked into the kitchen. DCI Hargreaves had wanted to take her home but she refused. Not because she wasn't nervous, she was, but she wanted him to get the surveillance on Night's house organised.

The forms were all saved on her hard drive, so all Hargreaves had to do was print them off again and get a team out there.

She opened the fridge and pulled two bottles of beer onto the counter. It was late morning, but she didn't care. Not after today, not after what she had been through. She knocked the cap off both bottles and took them to the bathroom. A long hot bath was what she needed. She hoped the beer would help her sleep. If not, there were another ten in the fridge that would definitely do the job.

She turned the taps on and lifted the first beer to her mouth. She grunted, the cold bottle both soothing and excruciating against her swollen lips. She kept it there though and downed half of it. She put the full one down beside the bath and carried the other to her bedroom.

She sat on the edge of the bed. She was wearing a set of grungy overalls, usually reserved for prisoners, and they were so long that they covered her feet and dragged on the carpet.

The paramedic had examined her but she wouldn't allow him to take her to hospital. He wanted to do an X-ray on her head to check her eye socket for possible fractures. The swelling was so bad the vision in her right eye had gone completely, and the swollen skin was stretched to its limits. Her mouth wasn't in great shape either. When the clown had brought his elbow up under her chin, she had bit into her top lip. It was also swollen and it made talking difficult.

Jane had barely recognised two members of her own team who came into the back of the ambulance to talk to her. She spoke to them calmly but despite having worked with them around the clock for the last week, she couldn't remember their names. She didn't mention that to anyone.

The female detective had taken her clothes and slipped them inside the evidence bags. The CSIs had taken photographs of her, and swabs from her hands and under her nails. She couldn't remember if she had scratched him but she just held her hands out for them.

And then Hargreaves had come in and knelt on the floor beside her. He was usually a no-nonsense, straight down the line detective but as she spoke, he became human. In the corner of his eyes, Jane saw tears forming. She reached out and took his hand but neither of them spoke for a while.

"I know you've already told Lenny and Lewis about it, but could you go through it again with me?" He released her hand.

Jane nodded and went through what had happened again. She could see Hargreaves wincing when she described hearing the knife cutting through White's flesh. Her voice wobbled when she told him about how White had screamed.

"I'll come back to the nick and write a statement." She shuffled off the trolley.

"No. No you won't," Hargreaves started. "I'll take you home and you'll sleep. Lewis made notes so the statement will wait."

Jane opened her mouth to speak, but she could feel her emotions betraying her and closed it before she started wailing.

"Anything else I need to know?" he asked.

Jane started to shake her head then stopped. She had been coming to see White to start the surveillance authorisation, but also to brief him on Stu's write-up of the rape. It suddenly seemed completely unimportant.

"Boss, I wrote up the surveillance authority but it was in my bag. If he knows what he's looking at, he knows we'll be watching Night." Each syllable stretched her mouth and made it sting.

Hargreaves stared at her for a moment without speaking. He was deciding what to do.

"Have you saved them?"

She nodded.

"Give me your password and I'll start the ball rolling. We've got nothing to lose and he might not be bright enough to realise what he's got in that bag."

Jane thought about her mobile and all the personal things on there. "I hope not."

"Have you got anyone who can look after you for a couple of days? Someone at home?" Hargreaves opened the rear doors of the ambulance, revealing a crowd of officers and CSIs moving quickly back and forth. Beyond them, Jane saw a bank of photographers and cameras pointing in her direction. At some point in the last few hours it had grown light and the vultures had descended.

"No, but I'll be fine."

He helped her down. "Sure? I can have a marked unit…"

Jane shook her head. There was no need for that. "Honestly, I'll be okay. I'll be back in the office in the morning."

Hargreaves led her to her car and stopped beside it. "We'll see about that. Keys?"

"In my bag," Jane replied. "I've got a spare set at home." It didn't really help matters now though.

He nodded. "No problem, I'll drop you off and bring your spare set back so someone can drop your car off. Plan?"

"I'm okay, really. You need to be here and I need that surveillance sorting as soon as. All I need is someone to take me home." She touched her eye and almost yelped. "I'm not going to be driving for a while anyway."

He'd looked at her and tried to smile. "This is shit, Jane. All of it is complete and utter shit."

She could hear the emotion in his voice. It sounded like he was about to crack up.

"We're going to get this bastard," she had said, looking toward the cameras and journalists. "I'm going to get him."

*

Jane lowered her body into the steaming bath. The water was so hot it nearly took her breath away; just how she liked it. She was exhausted, totally and utterly done in, her body aching terribly. Her legs felt like she had just done half an hour on the treadmill, and her biceps had done curls with weights that were double her usual maximum. She knew part of what she was going through was shock, mixed in with hunger, dehydration, lack of sleep, fatigue and stress. The latter factors were normal, things that she coped with on a daily basis. Not always that well, but she could cope.

But the shock was new. For such a small word, it carried a whopping punch. It had hit her harder than a clown's punch ever could. She had to regroup. Put her head and body back together before she would be any use to Hargreaves.

She slid forward, submerging her head. The water slipped effortlessly over her swollen eye and lips, soothing the constant ache. She could feel the heat gliding over her skin, trying to bring relief to her muscles. She could hear her heart beat. A steady, solid and dull thud in her ears. The water helped everything. It soothed, caressed and deadened the sound of the outside world.

But it couldn't muffle the sound of White's screams. It didn't lessen the sound of the clown's knife cutting through his flesh, grinding as it hit bone.

Jane rose to the surface, thrust her head over the side of the bath and relieved herself of the cold beer she had just drunk.

The water couldn't scrub those sounds clean any more than it could take the clown's crazy patchwork face from her mind. His smile which seemed to stretch so wide, almost from ear to ear, was made from bits of the men he had killed, from Newman, Stu and Crawley. And now there was one more slice of flesh on there.

She heaved again and climbed out, the brief enjoyment of the bath and the beer gone in an instant. Her legs felt like rubber as she stumbled against the sink. She held onto it for a moment and then cleared a small patch of steam off the mirror. Saw for the first time how truly bad she looked.

Each time the mirror steamed up, she wiped it clear. Again and again, leaning closer and closer each time. She looked wretched, almost as bad as the clown himself. He was connected to all of them: Newman, Stu, Crawley and White. She allowed her reflection to disappear behind the steam finally. But how was he connected?

She padded to her bedroom and fell onto the bed without drying herself. Was Night connected to them too? She pulled her legs up and lay on her side. It would all end with

Night, she was sure of that. Somehow it would all end with him.

She closed her eyes and wrapped her arms about her body. For the first time in her life, she wished there was someone there to hold her. To wrap his clumsy, untidy, noisy and affectionate arms around her until she fell asleep.

The pillow was already wet from her hair, but tears soaked into the fabric long after her hair had dried.

*

"Sarge?"

Jane walked through the office and sat down at her desk. She felt the eyes of all the officers fixed on her. She was angry with herself for being late but when she finally drifted off to sleep, she had slept like the dead; eighteen hours straight through. When she woke up cold and naked on her bed, she felt as if she had been run over.

"Are you okay?" She recognised Lewis's voice.

Jane held her hand up and tried to smile, but the balloons where her lips had previously been made it look like a grimace.

"Fine," she replied in a voice that wasn't quite her own. She wasn't fine, she was far from it, but that was what she was supposed to say.

She logged onto her computer. "Have I missed briefing?"

"Starts in five minutes."

Jane nodded and opened up the log of enquiries. It was growing by the second. As she scrolled down the screen, HOLMES populated the log with yet more queries. Even with a team five times as large, it would take years to work through them all.

She heard people leaving the office and slid her chair away to follow them. If she could make it through the day without crying or fainting, she'd be doing well.

Jane slid into the briefing room in the middle of the crowd. She wanted to avoid seeing Hargreaves for as long as possible. She had a feeling he might try to send her home and she didn't want that. The room wasn't particularly large but it was full, officers standing around the edge of the room. She filed in and stood beside an officer she had never seen before.

"There was no briefing yesterday for obvious reasons," Hargreaves began. "In my twenty-three years of service I have never experienced anything so… so… utterly shocking as what happened to John White."

I didn't even know his name was John, thought Jane.

"He hadn't been with us that long and it was probably the first time many of us had worked with him, but he was one of life's gentlemen, an honest, hard-working man with…"

Hargreaves paused and their eyes met. He looked away, back to the crowd. "He was just a good bloke."

There were a few murmurs of agreement around the room. More than there had been when White spoke about Stu. Silence had greeted his epitaph.

"But what we need to remember is that there's a job to do here, a really difficult job." Hargreaves walked to his computer and started a slideshow which played on a giant screen. He clicked through scenes that the officers all knew well: Harvey Newman's house, Stu Kelly's and Jim Crawley's. They were shocking images but everyone in the room was acclimatised to them, immune to the blood and the hellish mutilated expressions of those the clown had killed.

They swam across Jane's eyes like a nightmarish carousel. Her head spun.

Hargreaves paused the display and looked at her. He chewed on his lip for a second then continued. Even before the first image flashed up, she knew what it was going to be – the scene inside White's bedroom. Blood on the walls. Blood soaked into the beige carpet, turning it a muddy brown. His chair turned to face the mirror on the door of his wardrobe. The sparkle of a camera flash on the edge of the mirror. And in that sparkle, the ghostly image of a disfigured clown, laughing at her with that *oh-so-wide* grin.

She felt the image sliding away, sliding slowly off the screen and falling to the floor. Only it wasn't the image, it was her. She was the one who was sliding, falling away into the abyss of his diabolical smile.

She rubbed her eye and levelled herself with the sharp burst of pain it provided. She needed to get out, to leave the room before she was sick. She sidled out of the room, noticing only the slight turn of Hargreaves's head as he watched her, walked straight into the toilet and vomited her breakfast into the basin.

Her desk was at the far end of the office. To get to it, she had to walk past all the officers who had seen her leave the briefing. She managed only a dozen steps before Hargreaves called her.

"Jane? Have you got a minute?"

She stopped walking and closed her eyes. He was going to send her home, she knew it, but she was going to fight it.

She turned and tried to smile again before following him into what was White's office.

He waited at the door and closed it behind her. "I'd like you to go home, Jane."

He walked around the desk and sat down. He motioned for her to take a seat.

"It's too much. Finding Stu and then this, it's too much for anyone to cope with. Is there nobody who can stay with you? No…"

"Boyfriend? Partner? No, there's nobody," she interrupted to save him the embarrassment. "And I don't need anyone."

"Parents?" he persisted.

The thought of spending any period of time with them would drive her insane. "They live abroad," she lied. "Look, I really don't need to talk to anyone about it. This job sterilised me, emotionally, years ago."

He sighed. "Well whether you like it or not, you've got to have some form of counselling. It's policy but more importantly it *will* help. Whatever you say, Jane, I saw you yesterday, I saw what it did to you. What it did to me too, for god's sake. You can't just shrug this one off. It won't work."

"Will you let me stay if I agree?"

He smiled. "Are you kidding?"

"No," she replied. "I want to stay. I want to help."

He sighed again and shook his head. "Jane, you…"

"I'll stay out of the evidence chain. I'll sit over there and keep my head down."

He chewed his top lip. He was thinking it over.

"There's a link here, boss," she started. "And I want to find it. *I am* going to find it. Just give me free rein to work through it all."

She could see he wasn't sure. She wasn't in great shape, physically or mentally, but she was still better than anyone else he could bring in while she convalesced. She knew the investigation from top to bottom. If he did have to bring someone else in, it would be like starting from scratch. They didn't have the time for that.

"And if I throw up or pass out then I'll let you drive me home."

"How exactly did you get here this morning?" That was a good question. He was past thinking about her suitability to be at work, he was onto something new.

"Taxi. I've got my keys here, if someone could take me I'll drive it…"

"You're not driving anywhere. You can't see out of that eye, Jane. I'll have one of the team collect it."

She opened her mouth to argue, but if that was the only concession she had to make, she'd take it.

"You come to me with anything, okay? No going off on your own. Anywhere."

She nodded. She didn't want to go off on her own

anywhere, in the same way as she didn't want to be at home on her own.

"Are you running it now?" she asked.

Hargreaves nodded. "Yep. Saves bringing in another DI who doesn't know the case. It'd be like bringing in another DS, wouldn't it, Jane?" He winked at her.

She smiled, knowing it looked like a grimace, and turned around. "Oh, I nearly forgot." She turned back. "Surveillance?"

Hargreaves nodded. "Two teams. Ben Night is all tucked up and if he leaves, we've got another team standing by. If anyone goes near that place then we'll know about it."

"When did they go in?" she asked.

"I don't know exactly, but it was authorised at just after eleven yesterday morning. I'd say a couple of hours after that."

"Great." She opened the door and walked to her desk. She felt eyes on her again but ignored them and sat down. Somewhere in all this was the link. Somewhere in all this was a name.

20

Maldon huddled in the dark and pulled the hood over his head. It was cold, and his body ached from sleeping on a hard floor. At least he was safe. At least he was hidden. The music just kept on going around and around and around without pause or break. Note after note after note of *plinky plonk* out-of-tune clown music rattling around in his brain. It itched and it scratched and it was driving him insane.

"Turn it off, Sparkles," he whispered. "Turn the music off."

"You love it really, you lurrrrve it, don't try to deny it, Mouldy."

"Don't call me that," Maldon hissed.

He pressed his temple with his palms for as long and hard as he could but the music wouldn't quieten. If anything, it grew louder.

He reached into his pocket for the mobile phone; the one he had taken from inside her pocket, from that warm, cosy and gentle pouch on her thigh. He lifted it to his cheek and imagined it was her skin against his.

BOO!

Something spiked him and he nearly dropped it. Underneath the mask, he knew his skin was in a bad way. It felt strange, loose somehow, like beneath Sparkles's patchwork mask his own skin was dying. Was he dying too? Was this all the clown's plan? So he could take over completely?

He could feel huge volcanic spots erupting underneath the mask. In small areas, he could feel them trying to force Sparkles off his face. Little spotty defence mechanisms that were simply too weak to help. Small and weak, just like him.

None of it mattered anyway. He was Sparkles now. Sparkles the killer clown.

For a while he had listened to the police radio, holding it close to his ear with the volume on as low as possible. Listening to them talk to each other, he could imagine the panic they were all in. Rushing about like headless chickens, trying to work out in which direction he had gone. But he was already far away by the time they worked it out. Long gone.

Just as they found the burning car, the chatter stopped. Sparkles told him they had trackers on the radios and they knew where he was going, so he threw it in the river along with the bag and ran across the fields. He missed the voices and the strange beeping sounds the radio made. If only because it drowned out the constant loop of music in his head.

He pressed a button on the side of the phone. He had sat in the darkness for so long that the screen was dazzling and made him blink. A coastal image. In the foreground was a beach and waves, and in the background high cliffs rose steeply up to a blue, cloudless sky. He had never been to the seaside. He had never actually seen waves or stepped on sand in his entire life. And as for the sky, well, he never looked in that direction to see what colour it was.

He swiped his finger again and looked at the icons. They looked so colourful and cheerful, but she was probably like that too… happy, full of laughter. He touched the orange icon with 'Album' written beneath it.

"You don't want to look at that shit! We've got work to do!" Sparkles squealed, but he ignored him. It was getting easier to ignore his voice, if not his persistent music.

He scrolled through the images one by one, more than fifty before he found one of her. He was shocked to see how red her hair was. When she had attacked him, it had been dark and he hadn't taken much notice of the colour of her hair. He had been too busy trying to defend himself.

The photograph showed her at a wedding. Not hers by the look of it, but she was beside the bride and as the sun hit her hair, it sent sparks of red into the sky. It was like fireworks. He couldn't take his eyes off her beautiful hair. It was like nothing he had ever seen…

Only he had seen hair like that before, hadn't he? Someone he knew, someone special, had the same incredible hair. Someone he had loved. Love? Why had that word crept into his mind like that?

"Stop it, stop it, stop it!" Sparkles screamed.

Yes, he could see her face now. He could see her smiling at him, touching his cheek with a wonderful warmth.

He knew who it was now. His mum had red hair, just the same. And in the sunshine, in the garden at their house, the sun bounced off it and made fireworks in the sky too. He smiled and touched the screen until it went off for good. Then he put it in his pocket.

He looked up. Wafer-thin slivers of light like shooting stars jagged across his sky. They did little to illuminate the room but they told him whether it was night or day. By his reckoning he had been there for two nights, if you counted the remainder of the night after fighting with the red-haired police officer.

There had been noises from below. The sound of a single person wandering about a house, going about their business. There was the dog too. He seldom heard it but he had seen it before. He liked dogs but they never liked him.

He waited until he heard the sound of steps retreating down the stairs, then lowered himself out of the hatch. The house was far too large for one person to live in. It had too many unused and forgotten rooms. Rooms with loft hatches.

He lowered himself down and tried to listen for a sign that he had been heard. But he could hear nothing but the music and Sparkles whistling along to it. If you broke into someone's house and concealed the method of entry, they would never know you had been in there. That you were still inside. He would have to remember that. Not that there would be a next time.

He walked slowly toward the stairs, holding the knife by his side. The blade was rust-coloured now. Not from the weather but from blood. It seemed to weigh more after each use, like the blood was seeping into the metal. It was impossible but that was how it felt.

The lounge was empty and silent. He walked quickly to the kitchen. He knew where Night would be. Where else would a writer spend his days? He stopped halfway across the kitchen and stopped.

"Just turn the music off for five minutes," he whispered. "Please."

"Boring, boring, boring!"

"Now!" he hissed.

"Temper, temper!"

The music didn't go off completely but the volume decreased enough for Maldon to be able to think properly. He knew what he wanted to say and he wanted to get it right.

He continued across the kitchen and stopped outside the closed office door. Inside he could hear the sound of fingers rattling across keys; of words and worlds being created. It filled him with excitement.

There was also the sound of a dog growling. It was deep, low and threatening, And then the fingers stopped moving across the keys and he could stand at the threshold no longer. He hoped he wouldn't have to hurt the dog.

He opened the door and forced a smile across the mask.

"Boo!" he shouted.

21

Jane learned more about DI White in the next two hours than she had in the previous ten years. Hargreaves's reputation as being efficient was shown perfectly by the history he had already started building about White. He emailed it over without being asked. White had been married twice before and had two children. Thankfully, neither of the children lived with him.

It had taken yet more paperwork and several phone calls to get Social Services to release his career history to her. The manager she spoke to sounded close to tears when Jane told her the news about White. She had seen the report on the news and worked with him for several years before he left. She said their department was in shock. They all were.

Jane opened the electronic document and started reading. Now she had been given the time and space to work on her own, she wasn't going to miss a thing. Everything was there to be scrutinised. Everything.

White had worked in social care since leaving college. His

case notes were meticulous, as she expected, but there were so many it was impossible to go through them all. After reading a small cross-section, she grew morose. Not only was it like looking for a needle in a haystack but the subject matter was grim reading. Nevertheless she knew the needle was in there somewhere, she might just have to prick her finger to find it.

"How're you getting on?" Hargreaves was standing beside her.

She looked up at him. "So-so. Has Crawley's file been uploaded yet?"

"Should be on there." He paused and crouched down. "What links a paedophile clown, two coppers and a circus rapist? Sounds like it should be a riddle or a sick joke, doesn't it?"

Jane shook her head. "Before yesterday, it was Ben Night. But that link stops with White. They never met."

They talked about White and Stu without thinking about either of them too deeply. They couldn't afford to.

"He's still our best shot though. Just keep going, you're off the radar so to speak so make the most of it. Now, I've got some news that might interest you." Hargreaves stood up again.

"Go on."

"They might have found something on your suit. Well, inside a pocket to be specific."

"Pocket?"

"Who has access to your clothes, to the suit you had on yesterday?"

"Nobody. Just me. It's new so it's not even been dry-cleaned yet," she answered.

"There's a trace in there. Small but hopefully something."

"My phone was in my pocket, but he was wearing gloves. Latex gloves."

"Looks like he took them off and he's got a bad case of eczema."

Jane grimaced. She had been unconscious and completely vulnerable. He could have done anything to her and she would have been powerless to stop him, so why take his glove off to take the phone? She thought about his face again. The way his smile crept up toward his ears was almost child-like; the way a young child might try to draw a clown. A very creepy clown.

"When will we know?" she asked.

"It's at the top of the list so hopefully not too long. As soon as I know, you'll know."

Hargreaves walked back to his office, leaving Jane to her thoughts. Against her will, her mind created an image of the clown, dripping with White's blood, reaching into her pocket, touching her thigh, caressing it and…

She banged her fist on the desk to shake it off. The noise caused several officers to look over at her. "Tea anyone?" she shouted and walked over to the kettle.

*

It was dark outside and Jane was still going through White's file. She knew she was on borrowed time with Hargreaves.

The next time he came out of the office he would tell someone to take her home, whether she liked it or not. She couldn't go, though. Not until the DNA results were back.

It had taken her longer to read the documents than it would normally. She still felt tired and reading with only one eye took some getting used to.

Hargreaves's door opened. She hunched down in an attempt to hide but it didn't work.

"Jane, don't worry, you'll want to see this."

She straightened. "DNA?"

Hargreaves nodded and went back inside the office to answer a call. Jane jumped up and walked as quickly as she could across the office.

Hargreaves was talking on the telephone as she walked in and closed the door.

"I've got the Met doing a door knock now but I'm pretty sure he won't be there. Can I call you back in five, Steve?"

He said goodbye and hung up.

"We've got a name." He slid a sheet of paper across to her.

"Maldon Williams. Not a name I've heard of. Have we got an address?"

Hargreaves took the paper back. "Last known address is in London. I've got the Met looking at it but he isn't going to be there. Might find something useful in his flat though."

"What have we got on him?" she asked.

"Intel are producing a pack on him now." He drummed his fingers on the desk. "Are you up for it?"

"For what?" What was he asking her?

"A long night. I need you to find that link. I need to know where he's going next. I need to know why he's doing this. We need to stop this bastard, Jane."

She nodded. "I'll find it." She walked out of the office. She was going to find that link tonight, even if it meant staring at the computer monitor until the morning.

22

For a second, Ben was so shocked he froze. And then he thawed in a hurry and tried to jump up. The clown stopped him by stabbing the knife into the air an inch away from his face.

Stan growled and trembled. He put his hand down to soothe him. However unlikely, he didn't want Stan jumping up trying to attack the man. In this confined space, the dog would come off worse.

He stared at the clown and a minute passed in complete silence. He was able to take in what he was looking at. He stifled a scream. The clown's face was a patchwork of withered skin, gristle and dried blood. He reeked. Decay was floating off him like a festering miasma.

Their eyes were locked together as if they had both been hypnotised. Ben wanted to look away, to divert his gaze away from the beady lumps of coal that scrutinised him, but was completely transfixed by the monster. A real monster, not something he'd created with words.

At any moment, Ben thought he would be stabbed. Options were running through his mind. None of them were promising.

"What… do you want?" he finally uttered.

His words broke the spell.

"What do you want?" he shouted although he didn't feel as strong as his voice suggested. Stan whined.

"I am Sparkles."

"What?"

The clown was dressed in dirty brown overalls with splashes of white paint. A grim realisation struck him. The white splashes were the colour of the overalls. It wasn't brown, it was dried blood.

"Don't you think I look like him?"

Ben started to shake his head but he saw the change in the clown's eyes so he kept quiet.

"You threw my story in the bin." He took a step closer and Ben flinched. "Not good enough?"

He wanted credit for the story?

Ben felt sick. The inside of Crawley's caravan jumped into his mind. "Look, I know what you did to those others and…"

"This one will be better though because I'll be here with you."

Stan growled again and lurched forward. His jaws gripped the clown's bloody overalls at the ankle. Ben was so shocked all he could do was stare as Stan tried to pull the clown over. The moment was on him. *Act!* he thought and started to climb out of his chair. Sparkles raised his knife above his head. He was going to stab Stan in the head.

"Please, no!" he shouted and dropped on top of the dog, covering him. He heard the dog grunt and closed his eyes. There were no humans he would protect like this but Stan was more than that. He was better than any human he knew.

"Put him outside!" Sparkles shouted. His breath reeked, filling the room with a malodorous stench that was stomach-churning.

Ben opened his eyes. Stan was breathing beneath him. He kissed the dog's fur and gripped his collar. "I'll take him."

Sparkles allowed him past and Ben opened the door. "Go and have a wee, Stan," he said but the dog wouldn't go. He wanted to stay inside, with him. Maybe they could both make a run for it? Run across the fields and shout for help. But who would hear him? There was nobody for miles around. Ben got behind the dog and shoved him out. He would be safe out there.

"Back to the computer. Back to the story. To my story," Sparkles said softly.

He sat down and opened a new document. His hands were shaking as they waited for the first word.

"There was a boy…" the clown began.

Ben started typing. He used his skills to transcribe what Maldon said into a recognisable form. Into a story.

"Maldon, come inside and get changed, everyone will be here in a minute!" Mum called from the kitchen window.

He sprinted toward the house and jumped the two steps onto the patio. He was excited, really excited. Last night seemed to go on forever as he waited for the first sign of morning to filter through his curtains.

He bounded into the kitchen. "How long have I got?" he asked.

Mum was getting everything ready. He could see the sandwiches, the lemonade, and the crisps all laid out on the worktop.

She smiled at him. "Five minutes."

"I'll do it in three," he said and skidded off down the hall.

"Your clothes are out on the bed," he heard her call after him but he was already bolting up the stairs to his bedroom.

There were fifteen of his friends coming to the party. He had wanted the whole class but Dad said it was too many so he'd chosen his favourite fifteen. That was fifteen more presents to open!

He looked at the clothes Mum had put out. A shirt and a pair of jeans was not what he felt like wearing. He picked up the shirt and pushed it back inside the wardrobe. No chance he was putting that on.

The new England football shirt Dad had chosen was at the foot of his bed. That was what he was going to wear on his ninth birthday. He touched the embroidered badge. One day he was going to play for England and score the winning goal in the World Cup final.

Maldon pulled the shirt over his head and raced downstairs.

Mum and Dad were both in the kitchen. Dad had a can of beer in one hand and his other hand was on Mum's waist.

"What time is he coming?" Maldon asked.

Dad took a drink and smiled. "Now that would be telling, wouldn't it?"

Maldon nodded. "What time is it now?"

"Three o'clock." Mum turned around. "That's not what I put out for you. I wanted you to wear the shirt Nana bought you."

"It's his birthday, he can wear what he wants." Dad winked at him and Mum sighed.

The doorbell rang to stop any further discussion on the matter. "Looks like the first guest is here. Go and open the door, Maldon," Mum said.

He ran down the hallway and opened the door. His best friend, Mark, was standing with his mum. Mark had his England football shirt on too but it was last year's strip.

"Happy birthday!" Mark shouted and pushed a present at him. "Shall we go and play football?" he asked.

"I'll take that." Mum reached down and took the present off him. "See you at six," she said to Mark's mum.

Maldon led Mark toward the kitchen. "I've had a new football and goalposts," he said, "and when the others get here, we'll split into two teams. I want to be England."

Mark was always England when they played but now Maldon had the newest kit, he deserved to be them. Besides, it was his birthday.

"Okayyyy," Mark said and they ran onto the grass.

Twenty minutes later the garden was full of people, children and adults alike. Everyone who said they were coming was there, but the only irritation was that he had to keep on breaking away from the match to say hello to relatives. They were all laughing and enjoying themselves too and it was so loud with everyone shouting, screaming and laughing that he didn't want it to end.

He even managed to score two goals. It was perfect.

"Maldon, time for something to eat!" Mum's voice rose above the crowd.

Mum lay three large blankets on the grass and placed paper cups and plates down for everyone. Dad then brought out the food. There was an enormous tray of sandwiches, fives bowls of crisps, sausage rolls, cheese and pineapples on a stick, and peanuts. It was amazing.

"That should keep you quiet for a bit," Dad said as he left them to pour the lemonade themselves. It went everywhere, as was expected, but nobody cared. It was his birthday, the second-best day of the year. Christmas was number one and always would be.

"Happy birthday to you, happy birthday to you, happy birthday dear Maldon…"

His entire family came down the garden toward them and in the front Mum was carrying an enormous birthday cake. The breeze was only gentle but Dad was trying to shield the candles from it.

Mum put the cake in the middle of the blanket. "Blow them out and make a wish!" she said.

Maldon closed his eyes and wished that he was in the school football team, playing alongside Mark.

He opened his eyes and blew the candles out. The cake was a white square and in the middle was a replica of his new England shirt. The shirt had a number nine and his name on it.

"Nana made it," Dad said.

Maldon jumped up and kissed Nana. For a brief moment,

he wished he had worn the shirt she bought him.

Then from nowhere there was music. Maldon recognised it straight away and his excitement levels went up another notch. He could hardly breathe and his hands started shaking. It was circus music. It was the sound of clowns!

The crowd parted, and down the garden came a clown on a small bicycle. It was tiny compared to the clown and his knees banged into his chin with each pedal. He was incredible and for a moment, time stood still. The clown had silly, red flappy shoes, dazzling red trousers and a yellow top with bright red bobbles all the way down the front. His nose matched the bobbles for size but it caught the sun and shone like a ruby. His orange frizzy hair wobbled about on his head like a huge jelly. Maldon could feel laughter bubbling in his belly.

The clown went from side to side, seemingly out of control, and he laughed all the way past them until he drove into the apple tree at the bottom of the garden and fell off in a heap.

Everyone erupted into laughter.

"Did you see him? He went straight into the tree!" Mark shouted next to him.

Maldon had seen him, of course he had, but he couldn't speak. Some of the other kids thought clowns were for babies but he didn't.

The clown jumped up immediately and dusted himself off. He walked toward them. His smile was almost from ear to ear and just looking at him made Maldon want to laugh.

"Now then, who's the birthday boy?" The clown's nose was sunk in on one side. It had obviously been damaged in the collision.

BOO!

Everyone laughed again because the clown's voice was squeaky and high-pitched. He sounded like a cartoon character.

"Oh, I am sorry." He put his hand to his mouth and coughed. When he lowered his hand again, he was holding a small mouse. "I don't know how that got in there!" He threw the mouse at the group of boys and one of them shrieked. Maldon picked it up and laughed. It was rubber.

"Where was I? Ah yes, the birthday boy."

Maldon put his hand up and stepped forward. He was nervous but actually meeting a clown was something he would not miss for anything.

The clown crouched down so their eyes were on the same level.

"Your nose," said Maldon, "it's all squashed."

"It is? Can you fix it for me?"

Maldon smiled and nodded. He could feel his heart hammering away in his chest.

"I want you to hold my nose, close your eyes and wish as hard as you can for it to grow back. Can you do that?"

Maldon nodded, closed his eyes and put his finger on the shiny, red nose.

"Okay, everyone count with me. One… two… three!"

On the count of three there was a loud honking sound, which made Maldon jump back and open his eyes. Everyone was laughing and the clown was lying flat on his back.

For a second he was scared that he had hurt him but the clown sat up. This time his nose was three times bigger than it had ever been. It was enormous and it showed no sign of being damaged.

"Wow! You've got some powerful wishes there, Maldon!" The clown jumped up and walked toward him.

He offered his hand. "Happy birthday, Maldon. My name is Bingo and I'm very pleased to meet you."

The butterflies in Maldon's stomach danced around and around and it felt wonderful.

After only ten minutes, Bingo had mesmerised everyone there. He fell over, he made silly noises, he did some magic tricks that went wrong. One of them went so spectacularly wrong that he soaked the adults and then the children with water. Everyone at the party was laughing like mad and in the background was the crazy circus music, going round and round and round.

It reminded him of his trip to the circus with his dad. The whole audience had been roaring and Dad's beer had come out of his nostrils, he'd been laughing so hard. That was why he loved clowns so much. They made people laugh and laughing felt better than almost anything else he knew.

"Thanks for the present, see you at school tomorrow." He waved Mark, the last of his friends, off and his stomach tightened. It wasn't through excitement this time though, it was with sadness and disappointment. That was it for another year.

He felt a hand on his head and he looked up. It was Mum. "Don't be sad, the day's not over yet. Nana and Granddad are still here and your Uncle Russ. Come outside, I think Bingo is still here."

Maldon walked slowly through the kitchen and outside. The adults were sitting around a table laughing and drinking. The smell of cigarette smoke drifted through the summer air.

He jumped down the steps and walked to Bingo. The clown

was putting all of his things into a huge holdall. It looked big enough for him to climb inside.

"Did you enjoy the party?" Bingo asked.

"Yeah, I'm just sad it's over." He shuffled his feet in the grass.

"Me too."

Maldon lifted his head. "You are?"

"Of course! There's nothing better than making people smile."

"I suppose not."

"No suppose about it. If I could make you smile right now it would be the best feeling in the world." Bingo sighed and picked up his bag. "But you've seen all my silly stunts now. I've got nothing left. Would you pick that bucket up for me?"

Maldon reached down and picked it up.

"Would seeing inside my special clown van bring back that smile?"

He could hardly believe what he was hearing. He looked up at Mum and Dad. They were drinking and laughing with the other adults.

Bingo started walking away. "Better be quick or that smile will be gone forever!"

Maldon ran to his side. In his mind, he was already inside the van. There were hundreds of red noses hanging up along one side. A selection of different-coloured wigs on the other. There were hand-buzzers, rubber animals, bicycles, tricycles everywhere and the floor was a rolling mass of gobstoppers.

They walked through the house and out through the front door. And there it was, a plain white van with a picture of Bingo on the side. Beneath his picture it said, 'Bingo The Clown

– Tickling Ribs since 1982'. That was only two years after he was born.

"Doesn't look like much, does it? Just wait until you see inside. Come on."

Maldon followed him to the back of the van and Bingo opened it up. It was a huge disappointment. Inside there was nothing. It was practically empty. He threw the bucket in and turned around.

Bingo was standing a little too close to him and his eyes had changed somehow. He didn't look funny anymore. He looked scary.

"Boo!" Bingo said and pushed him into the van.

Ben felt tears building in his eyes. They were tears of anger and of sadness. He wanted to take Harvey Newman's face and keep punching it until there was nothing left but a bloody pulp.

"I'm glad you killed him," he said.

23

Jane walked down the corridor toward the exhibit store. She had put White's file away. Now they had a name, she wanted to start at the beginning and review what they already knew. It would be a long and laborious task, but if it stopped another murder then that was all that really mattered.

Ben Night's house was under surveillance and if anyone went near it, she would know. However much she enjoyed Night's first book, she wasn't sure she had the stomach to read any more. Not after what had happened yesterday. She looked at her watch. Pretty soon White's murder would be the day *before* yesterday.

She unlocked the room and pushed open the door. She waited for the motion detectors to trigger the lights before she stepped inside. The exhibit store had changed location several times during the last week. At first it occupied a box-room beside the main office. It moved to accommodate Stu's murder and then it moved once more to the current location. There were now three officers working out of the room and it was vast. It looked like a huge storage depot with computers, televisions, furniture and clothing all waiting to be shipped out.

She walked through the storage racks to the far end of the room. There were no windows this deep inside the building, so even in the daytime it was gloomy. At this time of night, the corner she was walking toward was covered in shadow. It contained all of the evidence from the first murder, from Harvey Newman's mutilation.

Jane paused as she reached his sordid little corner. There were computer towers lodged on the rack's lower level, and above them were his laptops and tablet computers. There were others too, others that the High-Tech Crime Unit were still examining. What she was interested in was stacked on the opposite rack, facing the computers.

It wasn't just his library of books that had been extensive. Harvey Newman had an extensive collection of videos, DVDs and flash drives too. The videos took up most of the room, neatly stacked side by side on the shelves. She marched straight past them without looking too closely and grabbed the book which the officers had created. Since none of the videos, DVDs or flash drives were labelled, they had catalogued and referenced them as comprehensively as was possible.

She scanned down the list, feeling more nauseous by the second. Beside each exhibit number was a name. The name of a child who Newman had abused. She knew what she was looking for and although she was relieved to find it so quickly, a wave of grief washed over her.

How many victims had there been? She had lost track in the wake of all that followed the discovery of his body.

She read the reference out loud and closed the book. "CR/12 – Maldon Williams." It was the exhibit number of the officer who found it and the name of the victim.

She walked back down the aisle and located the video. Its blank, black spine was as soulless as the man himself. She pulled it down and signed it out. A viewing room had been set up on the other side of the store. Did she want to see what was on the video? No, not with all her heart did she want to see it. Did she *need* to see it? She pushed the video into the player and sat down.

It was an old recording. The picture rolled over several times before it settled on the face of a young boy.

"Tell the camera your name," a faceless voice asked.

"I'm Maldon Williams," replied the boy. Whether it was because the footage was old she didn't know, but the boy's hair glowed almost white against the dark background.

"And why is today special, Maldon?"

The boy looked frightened to death and his voice wobbled. "It's my ninth birthday."

Jane calculated that it made the date the fourth of August 1989. She reached out to stop the video, she didn't need to know what happened next, but the camera moved and suddenly she was staring at a clown.

"Boo!" Harvey Newman smiled.

She stopped the video. In the silence, she could hear her heart hammering in her ears. It echoed in her head and around the room.

"Bastard!" she shrieked, smashing her fist into the desk. "Bastard, bastard, bastard," she shouted again. This time her anger wasn't directed at the killer of Stu Kelly or John White, it was directed at Harvey Newman.

She almost ran back along the corridors to the office. Her speed was as much about getting away from the cave-like room and the videos as it was about telling Hargreaves.

She knocked on his door and walked in. Hargreaves was just putting the phone down.

"Williams was one of Newman's victims." She felt dizzy and nauseous. "On his ninth birthday."

Hargreaves grimaced. "Christ." He threw his pen down and leaned back. "I've just had surveillance on the phone. They want to know if it's normal for Night to leave his dog out for nearly two hours. How the hell do I know?"

Jane shrugged.

"As long as nobody's been to his house, it doesn't matter. I'm not going to go and kick the door in over a damn dog."

Jane laughed, despite how she felt.

"Good work anyway. You okay?"

She didn't feel okay. She felt terrible. "Fine, thanks."

"Brings us back to revenge, doesn't it?" he asked.

Jane nodded. "Yes it does and who can blame him for wanting that? I certainly don't. It doesn't fit for the others though, not yet at least."

Hargreaves picked up his pen again and put it behind his ear. "Poor little sod." He started typing and Jane took it as a sign to leave. She needed to get back to her desk anyway. There was a drawer full of painkillers and she was badly in need.

24

Ben could hear Stan whimpering outside. The dog didn't like to be out in the dark for this long. Especially after recent events. But he couldn't move. Not only was the clown holding a knife covered in blood, but he was transfixed by the story he was transcribing. It made him feel sick, repulsed and sad. It made him feel angry.

"I went to school the next day like nothing had ever happened. I played football in the playground like normal and I ate my packed lunch as if I had never been in that van. I carried on like that for two weeks. Mum and Dad asked me why I was quiet but I just told them I was tired. I was angry with them too. I was angry that they had let Bingo do that to me. All the time I heard music. I heard the circus music playing over and over in a never-ending loop. But I knew nobody else could hear it. Only me. Just like I was the only one who could hear his voice. 'Don't tell anyone or they will take you away and you'll have to live with someone else. Someone mean. It's our secret, Maldon.'"

As he typed, Ben could hear the anger and spite in the clown's voice. It was strong. Why shouldn't it be?

"He took this," the clown said without any feeling.

Ben turned, watching the clown raise the knife and push the tip of the dirty blade into his face, into the part supposed to be a smile. The skin there was formed from someone else's face. The blade sank down deeper and deeper.

The clown laughed and withdrew it. The tip was covered in bright, fresh blood.

"But I've got it back now, haven't I?"

Ben turned back to the screen. The sound the blade made as it slipped through the flesh was repulsive.

"One morning I was sick. I was so sick I just couldn't stop it. It was everywhere. On my pyjamas, on my bed, on the carpet and even on the wall. Mum said I must have eaten something bad but I knew what it was. It was the secret. It was burning and boiling my guts. It was turning them to mush inside my body and if I didn't let it out I was going to keep on being sick. It was going to keep happening until my guts were covering all of the walls in the house. So I lay there and thought about how to tell them. I made myself sick again thinking about it and the day passed and the night came. But he knew what I was thinking. Just like he knows what I'm thinking now. He's in here."

Ben didn't need to look up to know the clown was pressing the tip of the knife against his forehead. He could hear it sinking into the flesh.

"I heard Dad come home from work. I could hear their voices in the kitchen and I could smell food cooking. I could smell meat roasting in the oven but I wasn't hungry. I walked downstairs knowing that I would puke at any moment. Seeing Bingo in my mind and hearing that music getting louder and louder and louder with each step. It got so loud that I couldn't hear them talking any more. I couldn't hear my own breathing or even feel my feet on the carpet. I didn't know whether I was alive or dead."

Ben struggled to keep up. His back was starting to ache from sitting there for so long.

"Mum had her back to me and Dad was sitting at the table reading his paper, smoking a cigarette. To the side of him was a window that looked out onto the garden. Only it was dark so I couldn't see out. I was about to tell them when he appeared at that window. He wrote the word 'Boo!' with bloody fingers on the window and smiled at me. The back door was open and he just slipped in. They didn't see him or hear him and I was too scared to say anything. I wanted to scream and shout and tell them what had happened but he had a knife. It was just like this one."

He was speaking faster and faster, and Ben started falling behind. He gritted his teeth and was about to say something when the clown just stopped speaking.

He typed the remainder of what he had just said then stopped too. The room was silent again. The only sound was from outside. Stan was whimpering. Ben risked a look up. The clown moved the knife moved up and down in a stabbing motion. Blood, his own blood, fell to the floor in a thick globule.

Should he move? Should he try and rush him?

"Pleeeeeease!" the clown whined. "I can't hear myself!"

Was he shouting at him? There was silence for a few minutes during which, Ben convinced himself, that he already dead and this was some kind of writers' hell.

"Bingo stabbed my dad in the neck first and then he stabbed my mum in the back and as she lay on the floor he slit her throat. Then he went back and finished my dad. He slipped out the same way as he came in. I saw his orange hair go wobbling past the kitchen window and he was laughing. He sounded just like Muttley."

He spoke calmly, as if he was describing what he had just bought at the shops.

"It all happened in the blink of an eye and I was powerless to stop it. I didn't even have time to scream. I'm not sure I had the strength to anyway."

Ben stopped typing. It was awful. It was all so unbearably sad. The vile disfigured animal standing with a knife in his hand beside him was also a victim. He didn't know what to think.

"Why have you stopped? Don't stop. Don't let the music start again."

Ben put in a page break and typed 'Chapter 2'.

"When the police arrived, I was standing in the same place. I was drenched in blood. It was even in my eyes and it was as if a red filter had been slotted in place. I watched everything through that red film. A copper threw up on the doorstep."

He paused and pulled a flake of loose skin off his hand. Ben watched it float to the floor like a feather. Both of his hands were covered in scaly skin which looked like it was ready to slough away at any second.

"They took me away and that was the last time I ever saw Mum and Dad. Two lumps of meat on the kitchen floor. A policeman took me into a room, a fat policeman with bad breath. I didn't know it then but he was a detective. I hated him. I hated the way he spoke to me, the way he drank his coffee and the way his voice sounded. He tried to make me look at photos of their bodies but I wouldn't look. He shouted all of the time but even his voice wasn't loud enough to rise above the clown's music. That was louder than anything for a long time afterwards."

"Are you talking about the same copper you killed?" Ben turned around slowly. He thought he already knew the answer.

The clown bent down so their noses were almost touching. The stench coming off him was unbearable.

"I took this back," he whispered.

Out of the corner of his eye Ben saw the knife moving inward, toward him, and he flinched. The clown pointed to a lump of flesh on his own jaw. It looked to have been painted or coloured red, just like the dollop of gristle he supposed was meant to be a big red nose. Close up, it all looked so child-like.

"All I could say was clown. Clown, clown, clown, clown, clown. Constantly, without stopping, and the music grew louder and louder. They gave me something to subdue me, knock me out, but even then my dreams were filled with clowns on little bicycles, talking with squeaky voices. Their smiles were upside down, just like mine. When I woke up, I was somewhere else. I was taken to a place where smiles weren't allowed and if you wore one, somebody else would come and steal it from you."

Maldon walked into the dining hall and looked around. It was two-thirds full already and the atmosphere felt charged with violence. There were other kids like him in here, kids without parents who were here by mistake. Then there were the others who wanted to be here. The one's who did everything they could to stay here. They built little empires around themselves and they filled it with weaklings and thuggish sycophants. He had been here long enough to know to stay away from them.

He liked to be on his own so he could listen to his music. It was music he didn't need headphones or batteries to listen to either. It just played on a continual loop and had never once stopped in six years. He liked to hum along to it too. But that was usually in his room in the dark when there was nobody else around. It was the only time he allowed himself an attempt at smiling.

Occasionally he got distracted and realised he had been humming aloud, but the other kids thought he was mad anyway. He didn't say anything to dissuade them of the idea.

The dinner lady slopped something that might have been cottage pie into his tray and he moved on. An apple and a plastic cup filled with weak orange squash. He knew what each element would taste like. They had tasted the same for years. He walked away and put his tray down on a table at the far end of the hall where a collection of frightened-looking boys huddled.

The cottage pie was grim, as it always was, but it reminded him of the same dish Mum used to make. Hers was...

"*So, you're Mouldy!*" *Someone was standing over him with a loud voice. This was how it always started.*

He carried on eating without looking up. He was aware that the other boys on the table had gathered their trays and were leaving.

"*Hey, Mouldy.*" *The boy pushed his tray.*

Maldon slid down the bench to reach his dinner. He hated being called that name.

"*I hear you're a bit of a musician, Mouldy.*"

It would either happen now, in a few minutes or next week but it was inevitable. He just wanted to eat his dinner.

"*I've got something for you.*" *The voice carried real threat now. It would be soon.*

Maldon looked up from his meal. The boy's cock was almost touching his nose. "*Try eating your dinner now.*" *He started pissing all over the cottage pie.*

For a moment, he was too stunned to move and his mind went back to being in the rear of the van...

"*Crawley's pissing on Mouldy's dinner!*" *A crowd had gathered and someone was laughing.*

Maldon stood up and shoved the other boy back. Urine flew off in all directions. The music went up to full volume in his ears.

Crawley didn't fall back very far and had already got his balance back. Maldon looked around, he was hemmed in on all sides. There was nowhere to go but if he could hold him off for a minute, a staff member might come and stop him.

Crawley launched himself forward. As he leaped, he punched Maldon in the mouth. He felt his teeth rattle and tasted blood. Then another punch hit him in his guts and he went down against the bench. He needed to get up. If he went down completely, he was done for.

He gripped the edge of the bench and tried to pull himself upright but another blow hit him on the temple. That one knocked him to the floor. He was barely conscious but the music was so loud he had no alternative other than to hum along.

He opened his eyes long enough to see the bottom of a boot come down on his face and knock him out completely.

"When he stamped on my head, the music stopped. I never heard it again until last week. Until I started wearing this."

Ben didn't need to look up to know he was pointing to his clown mask again. The name of the boy who stamped on his head hadn't gone unnoticed. Even then, Crawley had been a thug.

"I missed it," he continued. "I missed it because everything else grew louder. Especially voices. People spoke so loudly and I could hear everything they said. I didn't want to. I didn't want to hear any of it. The worst one of all was my social worker. He just wanted to talk and talk and talk."

"Do you miss your parents, Maldon?" White asked.
"What do you think?" he replied.
"I think you miss them very much."
"Well you're wrong, I don't miss them at all." He could feel anger bubbling away. It was just under the surface and that's

where it needed to stay. This was his exit interview. Everything was in place for him to move to London. To start again.

"It doesn't mean you're weak if you admit it."

Maldon sneered at him. He'd been in the system long enough to know that showing weakness was liable to get your head kicked in.

"I just don't think about them any more. Nine years is a long time." He thought about them every day. He thought about their gaping throats and the sound the knife made as it cut through their skin. And the blood. He thought about the blood a lot.

"What are you going to do when you get down there?"

"Work and sleep." There was a flat waiting for him. It was in a shared building and the job, in a chocolate factory, sounded like shit.

"That all?"

His voice was so loud. Why wouldn't he just shut up?

"Drugs, booze and prostitutes. Some of that too."

White sighed. "Say that to the wrong person and they won't let you go. Good job I know you so well."

How much blood would there be if he cut White's throat? From ear to ear, that would be the way to go with him. God, he wished the music would come back. Then he could just tune out of this shit and relax.

"Bingo."

Had White just said that? "What?" Maldon asked.

"Nothing. I didn't say anything," White replied. He looked confused.

"You did. You said... You..." But he couldn't bring himself

to say the name. "You should watch what you say to people."

"Why? What do you mean, Maldon?"

Because I'll stab you in the fucking face with a pen if you say that name again, he thought.

A knock on the door and a woman poked her head around. "The car's waiting."

White stood up. "Have you got everything?"

Maldon nodded and picked up his bags. He stared at White for a moment and felt relief. He wouldn't have to jump through any more hoops or talk about his parents to this man ever again.

White broke eye contact and offered his hand. "You know where I am if you need me."

Maldon ignored the hand. "Oh, I know where you are."

He walked out of the door.

"And I didn't smile or laugh for twenty years. It's just not been in me. Know what that's like?"

Ben shook his head. It felt like a very long time since he had laughed or smiled. Maybe even years. But twenty? Nowhere near. What would it be like to lose such a huge part of humanity like that?

"That guy stole the last trace and ate it. That's what that sort of person does. They take it all away. Newman, the copper, Crawley and the social worker. They took it all and left me with *nothing!*" He screamed and stabbed the knife into the desk, just missing the keyboard.

Ben jumped to the side. "What did I do?" he shouted. The words forced out of his mouth by panic.

The clown withdrew the knife. It left a stab mark in the

wood like a cut, surrounded by drops of blood.

"You? You helped me get it back." His voice changed in an instant. "You sent me the book. You told me what I needed to do to get my smile back. I had to take back what they had stolen from me. The only way to do it was to become Sparkles."

"It's just a book," Ben whispered.

The clown rummaged underneath his overalls and brought out a copy of Clownz. "Will you sign it for me?" He dropped it on the desk with a dull thud.

Ben looked at it and then back at the clown. Was this happening? Was it really happening to him?

"Here's your pen."

He took the pen from the clown's hand and opened the book. His hand was shaking but not enough to stop him signing his name.

"Make it out to Sparkles."

He could feel, and smell, the clown close to his shoulder. He signed it and closed the book.

"I read it the first time in prison. And in that week I read it four times. I hid it in my gear when they released me and I've had it ever since. It's the most incredible…"

He stopped mid-sentence. Ben looked up. All around the mask were cuts where he had been stabbing himself. And out of these cuts, trickles of blood were running and painting the mask. The clown looked to the ceiling and screamed.

"Noooooooo! I can't hear him! I can't hear him!"

Ben forced himself as far way as he could. His chair crashed against the window.

"It's too loud! I don't want to hear it any more! Pleeease! Stop the music!"

The knife was slashing through the air just a few inches from his face. If he moved it would cut him to ribbons.

"It's my story. I have told him everything!" The clown was swaying back and forth in some sort of trance.

"Please," Ben muttered.

"I don't want to think about them any more!" The clown roared and stabbed the knife into his cheek.

"I'll cut you off! You'll never make me think about them. You'll never make me…"

Ben watched as the clown started cutting at his face.

"I won't do it. I won't tell him!"

Blood flew across the computer screen.

Ben jumped up and grabbed his wrists. "No!" he shouted.

25

"Shit," Jane whispered. The roar in her ears was deafening.

"Boss!" she shouted. The office was empty now. There was just the two of them here. Why wouldn't there be, it was after three in the morning.

"You want me?" Hargreaves walked out of his office.

Jane looked up. "Pull up a chair."

"That good, eh?" He wheeled a chair toward her.

She turned the screen so he could read it easier. "I'm not sure good's the right word." She let him read in silence.

After five minutes he looked up. "Shit." He looked back at the screen. "Why didn't we know about this?"

Jane shrugged. "It's before our time. Stu wouldn't have had that much service by then."

Hargreaves sighed and leaned back. "Surely he would have mentioned this." He tapped the screen.

"He was pissed most of the time. I doubt he wanted us rummaging through his old case notes either."

"Christ." Hargreaves rubbed his eyes.

Jane turned the screen back around so she could see it. "I've got to go through this again," she said.

As she started reading, she could picture everything Stu had written. It played out before her in vivid detail. The summary report was far more impactive than the long-winded statement which was attached. This report told her everything she needed to know.

> *Report of DC 1209 Kelly*
> *Incident 761*
> *At 21.05 hours on 7th August 1989 I was on duty, single crewed, as the Night Crime Car. I attended 12 Wilson Croft, Derby following a report of domestic disturbance at the address.*
>
> *On attendance there were no replies to either knocking or repeated shouts from myself at the front and so I walked to the rear of the property. As I approached the back door I saw there were lights coming from inside and so knocked on the door.*
>
> *There was no reply and the back door had frosted glazing at the top preventing any view of the inside. I could detect no signs of disturbance coming from inside.*
>
> *I called out several times, with words to the effect of, "Police, can you open the door please," without response.*
>
> *Due to the nature of the call I walked past the door to the window and looked inside. Immediately I saw there was a considerable amount of blood on*

the floor and walls and ceiling. I also saw a man sitting at the table. He was slumped forward with his forehead resting on that table.

As a result I took a rock from the garden and used it to smash the glazed part of the door and reached inside to turn the key.

Once inside I ran directly to the man. A large amount of blood had pooled on the floor beside the table where he was slumped. Blood also covered the table. I checked his pulse and saw the wound to his throat. It had been cut open from below his left ear, extending all the way to behind his right ear. There were no signs of life, although his body was still warm. A newspaper was on the table in front of the man. It was illegible such was the amount of blood.

I left the man and looked about the room. At that point I saw a female lying on the floor in the kitchen at the other end of the room. Blood covered her body and the floor around her. I ran forward and slipped, falling to the floor beside her.

The female was on her right side and I could clearly see the wound on her throat. It was in a similar fashion to the male. Her neck had been cut from one side to the other.

At this time I looked around for a telephone and saw in the doorway to the kitchen the boy I now know to be Maldon Williams. He was wearing a clown's mask.

He said, "Boo!" and then smiled at me. The mask

was covered in blood, as were his hands, clothes and the blade of the knife. Droplets of blood fell from his nose.

I asked him if he was injured. His reply was "Boo!"

At this time I also saw he was holding a large carving knife. I asked him to put the knife on the floor. He looked at the blade and then at his parents and the blood. He laughed.

I asked him again and this time he dropped the knife to the floor and shouted "Boo!" On this occasion it was much louder. He continued shouting in this manner until he was taken out of the address by the paramedics despite my efforts to make him stop.

My original statement is attached.

Stu's report didn't get any easier to read the second time around. There was more too. Findings, evaluations and assessments, and all of them came back to the same point.

Maldon Williams had murdered his parents.

They didn't know that Newman had molested him back then. How could they? Maldon never told anyone.

She heard Hargreaves's phone ringing in his office. She hadn't noticed him leave her. He came out a few seconds later. "They're saying the dog's been out for nearly four hours now. Should we be worried, Jane?"

There was no way of knowing what Night's routine was, but the dog didn't look like he was normally left out all night.

"They're saying it's going mad. Barking, whining and scratching at the door. It's running from front to back constantly. There's a small window at the back of the house and the light's on, has been since it got dark."

"That doesn't sound right." She looked at the report on the screen. Her eyes felt like they were full of razor blades. "Fancy a drive out?"

Hargreaves frowned. "At this time of night? He'll either be fast asleep or drunk."

Whether it was the report she had just read or something else, she felt on edge. She needed fresh air and to stretch her legs. It wouldn't take long to get there and back.

"When was the last time you went out on an enquiry, boss?"

Hargreaves ended the call and went back in his office to fetch his coat. "Let's go."

It was only a short drive from the city but it felt like a different world. Jane looked at the dark houses as they drove past. After this week, a change of scenery might be just what she needed.

Hargreaves pulled onto the track leading to Night's house. All the time, he was talking to the surveillance team on his mobile. Jane kept her eyes on the hulking shadow of the house as they got closer. From this angle, she could see no signs of life.

He put the car into neutral, switched off the lights and coasted the last fifty metres. His tyres crunched on the gravel surface of the track.

"What do you reckon?" he asked.

They both looked at the house. "No harm in knocking. I'll say we were just doing the rounds and wanted to make sure he was okay," Jane replied.

They both climbed out and walked toward the door. "Looks like he's doing all right for himself anyway." Hargreaves nodded at the house.

"Was. *Was* doing all right," she said in response.

Stan came trotting around the house and ran straight to her. He wagged his tail and chattered his teeth. "Hello, boy," she said and stroked his head. As well as a change of scenery, a dog might be a good idea. It had to be better than having a man in the house.

She banged on the door and waited. There was no response. Hargreaves stepped back to look up at the front bedroom. "Nothing."

Jane banged again and still there was nothing. "Back?" she asked.

Hargreaves shrugged and followed her.

26

Maldon's hand was steady as he dragged the knife across his cheek. He felt the air caress his flesh, his own flesh for the first time in days.

"You can't get rid of me, you daren't, you big scaredy-cat!"

Sparkles was screaming and wailing. His high-pitched squeal rising above the music. The music was slipping away into a jumble of notes now. It was almost unrecognisable as his beloved tune.

He stepped back, away from Ben and his grasping fingers.

"Stay where you are!" he ordered.

"Oooh hark at you, big, brave and bold now, aren't you! Well you're only like that 'cos I taught you how to do it. You weren't like that in the back of Bingo's van…"

"Shut up! Shut up, shut up!" Maldon screamed and hooked a lump of flesh off his face. It fell to the floor silently. Ben stepped toward him again. He was mouthing something but his words fell silently, like the slice of Bingo's face he had just hacked off.

"Stop, you're hurting me!"

"You told me I'd get my smile back! You told me if I killed the men who stole it I'd get it back. Only I haven't, I haven't got anything back. You lied to me. You lied just like Bingo!"

"Kill the writer, that'll do it. Kill him and we'll sit at the table and eat his brains. You'd be a writer then. A smiling writer!"

"No, you're a liar. You can't give me anything!" Maldon screamed and it was louder than he ever thought his voice could go. The knife reached beneath the mask and pierced his own flesh. Warm blood flowed down his wrists. It felt no different to the blood of the others he'd killed. It shocked him. Shouldn't it feel different? Wasn't his blood somehow distinct to theirs?

"Please!" He heard Ben's voice now. "We've still got to write the final chapter. It's not done yet. Your story isn't finished. *Your* story, Maldon, not Sparkles's story, not anyone's but yours. It's not finished! I can't write it without you."

The writer looked at him. On his cheeks were tears. Who were they for? For him?

"Kill him, Mouldy, kill him dead. He's right, you're not finished. Kill him!"

Sparkles's voice was fainter. Fainter than it had been, at least. He flicked a piece of flesh away. He saw the black diamonds rotate in the air and land by the writer's feet. Why should he kill him? Why did Sparkles want the man who created him dead? It made no sense. No sense at all. He kept cutting.

"Stop! No!" Ben jumped toward him, reaching for his wrists. Holding his slick wrists with his own hands. His writer's hands. The same hands that had written all those books and taken him out of his own mind to somewhere else.

His wrists were slippery though and Ben's hand kept falling away from him. Sliding down the blade, cutting him across his arm. No, this was wrong. He didn't want to hurt this man. He just wanted Sparkles gone.

The writer stepped away from him, holding his own hand, blood dripping to the floor and grimacing in pain.

"I'm sor…" he started.

"Hahahahahahahahaha! Can you hear that, Mouldy? It's laughter, it's real laughter, makes your tummy feel funny. You did it before…"

But it didn't sound like laughter. It sounded like a child screaming. A child screaming deep, deep down where nobody could hear it, strangled and tortured. His own screams.

He held his face with one hand and started slicing through Sparkles This time he'd slice right to the bone –

"Police! Drop the knife, Maldon!"

He turned toward the door. The police officer was there. The lady with the red hair, just like his mum's. She knew him too. She knew his name. His mum, his beautiful mum. She was gone. They all were now.

"Maldon, please. We know what he did to you. We know."

Her voice was soft and gentle. He recalled how warm her

skin had been when he'd touched her. How the photographs on her phone had shown the sun flickering through her hair. How it had made flames and fireworks. Just like Mum's.

He pushed the knife under his other eye and flicked away the final piece of the clown's mask. The final black diamond was gone, and as it spiralled to the floor a thin, reedy voice bounced off the walls in his mind.

"Hahahahahahaha. Hehehehehehe."

Then it was gone. And so was the music.

He dropped the knife. It fell to the floor, the tip of the knife piercing the last piece of Harvey Newman's face.

He could hear a voice calling for help, calling for an ambulance, but all he felt were the arms of a woman who looked and smelled like his mum. A strange feeling fluttered around his stomach, rose up through his chest and into his throat. It flowed out of his mouth and tickled his cheeks.

One corner of his blistered lips twitched. A smile. The beginning of a smile.

27

Ben looked out of his office window and counted the chimney pots he could see – around ten. At least ten people who lived within striking distance. The new house had plenty of neighbours. That was better than not being able to see anyone and nobody seeing you.

A year had passed since Maldon Williams, and everything had changed. Everything.

"Nearly finished?" Jane asked and kissed the top of his head.

"Not far off, another ten minutes and I'll be done."

Former Detective Sergeant Jane Brady had moved in three months ago. It was then that he lost Stan. As it turned out, Stan was a ladies' man, rather than a man's man.

He was writing too. Writing more in the last six months than he had done in the last five years. The scar on his wrist itched like crazy some days. It would never allow him to forget Maldon, not that he would ever try.

Maldon had been taken away to a secure clinic where he

would never be a danger to himself or anyone else. His tragic life would end in that place, but Maldon would know nothing of it. His mind had locked itself into some alternate reality. Where or when it was, nobody knew for sure. But when Ben was eventually allowed to visit him, the perpetual, locked-in smile on his face told all.

He tilted his head back and puckered up for a kiss. "Ten minutes, I promise."

She kissed him. "Why does it always smell like feet in here? Feet that haven't been washed for a week."

He laughed. "That's my brain burning up."

She patted her leg. "Come on boy, let's leave him to his smelly socks." Stan followed her out and she closed the door behind her.

After Maldon had been taken way, or most of him had been removed, Ben had sat quietly in his office staring at the screen. He could think of nothing else to do except write. The only problem was, he had no idea what he was going to type.

And then it came to him. Or rather, he saw it. Under his desk, just at the joint between the side and the back, was a strange-looking lump. It looked like spat-out bubblegum and he was about to get annoyed that one of the officers had left it behind.

He had bent down to pick it up. It didn't feel like bubblegum. It felt like something else entirely. It was human flesh. It wasn't as bright red as Sparkles's nose on the cover of the book but that's what it was. A clown's nose. A part of the mask nobody except him knew about. .

Remembering that day, nearly a year ago, Ben fished into his pocket and touched it. It was part of Maldon, it had to be. Oh yes, he knew exactly who to thank for his burst of creative energy.

He smiled and started typing. There would be no clowns in this story. Not a chance. He always wanted his books to have an impact but Clownz had been destructive too. He knew of two men whose lives it had helped destroy; two men it had transformed into monsters. He couldn't and he wouldn't write about clowns ever again.

There was a witch in the story, though. A vile, bed-hopping, spell-casting, wart-infested bitch of a witch who enjoyed making men's lives a misery.

He had her name before he'd even started the story. A pleasant-sounding name, if a touch unusual. The witch was named Fleur. He had her end worked out too. He was going to enjoy writing that. Oh yes, he was going to enjoy describing that in gory detail.

This one was going to be the best book yet.

The End

Printed in Great Britain
by Amazon